A Spirited Swindler

A Midlife is Murder Paranormal
Cozy Mystery
Clare Lockhart

Apatite Publishing

For John Burrows, my best friend and partner in every universe.

Also by Clare Lockhart

Midlife is Murder
Paranormal Cozy Mystery Series

Midlife is Magic
Paranormal Cozy Mystery Series

Dear Reader,

I want to thank you for reading this book and welcome you to the Midlife is Murder Paranormal Cozy Mystery Series and to the imaginary small town of Bookend Bay nestled on the sandy shore of Lake Superior.

In this series, you'll meet Quinn Delaney, a newly divorced, amateur sleuth who's going through a few changes. Some are welcome (an empty-nest and opening of her dream café) and some not so much (a sudden ability to see ghosts, an OCD twin from a parallel universe, and a rash of murders).

If you like reading about best friends who find themselves in the odd pickle yet persevere until they've caught the bad guys, then you're in the right place.

If it turns out you enjoy spending time with Quinn in Bookend Bay, I invite you to join my newsletter on my website **https://clarelockhart.com** and get a free novella in the series and learn about my Midlife is Magic series.

Happy reading!

Love and hugs,

Clare

Chapter One

As I stood on the boardwalk that ran through Courtesy Park, I sensed with a prickly certainty that I was being watched. With orchestrated casualness, I glanced around me.

About thirty feet away, a blonde woman stood behind a bench, staring in my direction. Gooseflesh trickled along my arms, but I wasn't chilly. It was an unseasonably warm May afternoon.

I narrowed my eyes and met the woman's biting gaze. She was vaguely familiar. Maybe I'd seen her an hour ago at the music shop, but I couldn't believe she'd follow me to the park. Who would follow a mundane, peri-menopausal, married woman, emphasis on *mundane*?

Maybe I was imagining things, and she was watching the boats in the bay behind me. She might even be wondering why I was now staring at her.

I returned my attention to my brand-new café—Break Thyme—opening in three and a half weeks. Hallelujah!

I'd been envisioning opening day for much of the last three years when I started to seriously redefine my role as a homemaker and determine what to do with myself when our nest emptied. Full of energy, I wanted a job where I could be my own boss and draw on my skill set—I was a good cook, multi-tasker, organized, loved to socialize, and create new drinks. When I'd complained to my best friend Toni about the lack of good quality coffee in Bookend Bay, she suggested I open a café where I could also sell my specialty achohol-free beverages. I could call them *artisan.* The idea took hold in my mind and grew until it felt exactly right. Then I took that dream and made it happen.

And here I was. Three and a half weeks until opening day. I blinked away a tear and swallowed. This felt like the most significant thing I'd achieved, besides raising my two children, and this creation was all mine.

A movement in my peripheral vision broke my concentration. I looked in the strange woman's direction to see the fluttering of her saffron scarf, but there was no breeze. I remembered that scarf. Yes, I was sure of it now. She *was* the same woman from the music shop, and she was still staring my way.

A phone started to ring. Mine, I realized. My mother's ringtone. I kept one eye on the woman, although she didn't look dangerous, and reached inside my purse. Mom now lived in Nova Scotia. She'd moved back to her Canadian roots after Dad died eight years ago.

"Hi, Mom. How are you?"

"Well, dear, I'd be much better if most of my friends weren't hoodwinked this morning." Her voice was tight, almost shrill.

My chest filled with dread. My mother rarely tended toward dramatics. "Oh, no. What happened?"

"I've been hacked! Some hobnocker emailed all my friends, pretending to be me. They said I needed money to buy my granddaughter a birthday gift."

What could I do? Criminals had targeted my mother, and I didn't know how to help. Living fifteen hundred miles away sometimes had me feeling useless, an uncomfortable sensation for someone who liked to think of herself as practical and resourceful. "Oh, Mom. No wonder you're upset."

"Can you imagine me asking my friends for money? What must they think? I've been on the phone for the last hour. Everyone is calling to see if it's true." I felt for my mother, whose pride in her thrifty ways and financial independence would never have her asking for money. Mom said her greatest achievement was stretching Dad's meager salary at the fish processing plant far enough to serve three square meals a day, save pennies, and grow a hardy retirement fund.

"I'm sorry this has happened to you," I said. "The saving grace is that people are aware of these scams nowadays. Your friends will know you'd never ask them for money."

She scoffed. "I just got off the phone with Myrtle. She couldn't get through to me with everyone calling. That scammer, the no-good son of a motherless goat, told her to buy gift cards—two hundred dollar's worth. And she did it! Marched right over to the drugstore and dropped down her money."

My heart sank, but I was also relieved it was only two hundred dollars. "How could Myrtle fall for this? She's an intelligent woman." Myrtle, a retired mathematics teacher, was one of the most fiscally savvy people I knew. Her years of corralling hormonal teenagers in her classroom also made her wise to tricks and attempts at foolery.

"I don't know. I'm some surprised, all right. The scammer asked Myrtle to email a code from the gift card to them so they could cash the card right away. They said they'd pay her back on Wednesday."

"Oh, no. Mom, you need to email all your contacts and warn them."

She sighed. "My contacts are gone. Every last one of them. The scammer deleted them all."

"What? They can do that?"

"I suppose they can since they did."

"Right," I said. I drew a breath and let it out slowly. My mother was pretty tech-savvy for a seventy-seven-year-old, but something like this was beyond both of our skill sets.

"I'm just sick about this," she said. "I don't know what to do."

"I suppose you should call the police. And I'll give Jordan a call. He should be able to help with this." My son Jordan was an *ethical* hacker—believe me, it took me a long time to reconcile those two contradictory ideas. Businesses hired him to break into their computer systems to find vulnerabilities, so if anyone would know how to retrieve her email contacts, he would.

Her groan sounded in my ear. "I have another call. Oh, fish paste! It's my mechanic. He must have gotten an email, too. I just want to wring someone's neck! What are people going to think of me?"

"Remember, it's not your fault. I'll talk to Jordan and call you later."

She said a quick goodbye and disconnected. Since Jordan was working, I sent him a text.

Heaving a sigh, I shoved my phone back in my purse and looked to see if the woman was still there. She was, and the direction of her stare hadn't changed. I looked behind me, but there was nothing to see in her line of sight.

This woman was making me uncomfortable. I adjusted the strap of my leather purse and walked toward her.

As I approached, I saw she didn't look well. Thin blue veins crossed over her jaw from her neck. A mole stood out under her left eye. Her skin was pale enough to suggest an illness. Still, healthy or not, she was beautiful. Bombshell came to mind. Blonde hair, not one astray, fell in waves just past her shoulders. She wore a tight, flowery, low-cut dress showing off an ample bosom. Her gaze was most definitely on me.

I ran my fingers through the ends of my shoulder-length hair, reminded of the gray strands among what used to be shades of mahogany. "Can I help you with something?" I said, stopping in front of the bench. I moved my hand to my hip. Power pose. "Did you follow me here from the music store?"

She looked surprised for a split second, then lifted her chin and cast her eyes over me in what might have been superiority, but since it wasn't polite to make assumptions, I gave her the benefit of the doubt. Still, I stood up straighter when her gaze flicked from my head to my runners. "Yes, you can help." Her tone wasn't all that friendly for someone wanting assistance.

Obviously, a stranger because courtesy was a theme here in Bookend Bay. Many of our streets were virtuously named like Mercy, Humility, and Tolerance. Folks around here believed in the nobler of the Golden Rules, as opposed to my husband's version, *he who has the gold rules.*

"You are Quinn Delaney," she said. It wasn't a question.

I searched my memory for how I might know her and came up blank. "I am. Have we met?"

She shook her head. "No. I'm acquainted with your husband."

My husband? I felt a quiver in my stomach before having the reassuring thought she could be a business associate or a client of the bank where Bryan managed estates and trusts. But then why didn't she say so? Why did I feel like I had to pull information from this woman who seemed to want something?

"How do you know Bryan?" I asked.

"We met, about a month ago, at a funeral," she said.

I thought back, remembering a colleague of Bryan's who'd been tragically hit by a car while he was jogging. I'd never met the man and couldn't remember his name. Bryan had attended the funeral alone. My impatience dropped a notch at the mention of the death. Maybe this woman was still grieving and that was why she was acting strangely.

"And you are?" I asked.

"Beverly Foster." She made no move to come around the bench, so I stayed where I was. Having a bench between us gave me comfort, although I wasn't sure why I felt in need of security in the middle of the park in broad daylight.

I waited for her to continue. When she didn't, I asked her what she wanted.

"I'll tell you where to find a set of keys, then I want you to get in touch with a woman—Hannah Wyatt. We'll go from there. Simple as pie."

I stared at her. Dumbfounded, then I laughed, a more nervous sound than I'd have liked. She must have been joking. "Very funny. Why in the world would I do that?"

She smiled, but not in a warm or friendly way. Not exactly malicious either. It seemed more like she was mocking me, as if I'd just said something ridiculous and she knew much better. My patience snapped. What kind of game was she playing?

"Because in exchange, I will give you the evidence you'll need to absolve your husband."

A jolt of alarm ran through me. "Absolve him of what?"

My phone rang, giving me a start. I grabbed it from my purse, then glanced at the screen. My mother's call, again, and with it came a reminder there were scams in the air. I would not be victimized. It was time to give stalker-lady a piece of my mind. I turned away from Beverly Foster to answer my phone.

"Mom, can I call you right back?"

"It happened again!" my mom cried. "One woman from my church group just called to ask if I got the gift card she bought. Another two hundred dollars!"

"Okay, hold on. I need ten seconds to finish something here." I turned back to the bench, but Beverly wasn't there. I spun around. Well, spun might be overly gracious. The spurious bombshell was nowhere to be seen. Where had she gone so quickly?

Unfortunately, my trepidation didn't vanish completely with her. My stomach muscles clenched, and I knew it wasn't the egg burrito I'd had for breakfast.

I shouldn't let this worry me. Shouldn't think the worse and get fooled into questioning whether Bryan had done something wrong. No, that woman had tried to pull one over on me and must have thought better of it. Or she was bonkers and ran off to find someone else to harass.

There was nothing to worry about, I told myself again. Bryan would have told me if he was in any sort of trouble.

Chapter Two

I'D ALMOST FORGOTTEN I had my mother waiting on the phone. Pushing aside the emotional chaos Beverly had triggered, I listened to and sympathized with my mom. She felt responsible for her friends' losses, so I firmly reminded her she wasn't at fault. By the time we hung up, I'd talked her out of repaying the people who'd fallen prey to these scumbags, reminding her again it wasn't her fault she'd been hacked.

What a strange coincidence for both of us to be managing scammers at the same time. The more I thought about it, the more I was sure Beverly intended to rip me off with some creative scheme and had lied about Bryan. We'd been happily—okay, contentedly—married for too many years for me to doubt him because some stranger planted seeds.

This moment was supposed to be special for me, so I turned my attention back to my café to take in the new sign that now hung over the French doors to the patio, while a replica of the sign hung at the front entrance on Courtesy Boulevard. An elegant script spelled the words Break Thyme set in a lightly hued, aqua-marine wreath of thyme with a mug and glass above and the words *Artisan Beverages and Treats* underneath. Perfect. Just as I'd envisioned.

The sight made me so darn happy. Like a five-year-old, I wanted to skip and sing.

From this vantage, I could see most of the twenty or so shops that ran along Courtesy Boulevard. The back of each shop faced the park and Lake Superior. These charming lakefront shops were prime locations here in Bookend Bay. And I'd snagged one. Dropping off a jar of my Ginger Lime Thyme Jelly to Lottie, a local realtor, sure paid off when she contacted me before the property was listed. Since my finances were in order, I got the lease.

The view from Break Thyme's patio was spectacular. As well as the lake, my customers could also see the two majestic rock spires that bookended the river mouth where it met the great lake, hence the name of our small town—Bookend Bay.

My phone pinged with a text. Seemed like I was in high demand suddenly. It was from my husband Bryan. *Can you be home at 5:00? Something important to discuss.*

Oh? I typed back, feeling a return of the nerves sparked by the conversation with that strange woman. *Sure. Something good, I hope?*

See you then.

Okay, well, that was abrupt. He must be busy at work, probably in between meetings with clients or management. At forty-nine, I was old enough to know that worrying would not solve this problem, so I stopped thinking about it and headed to my truck.

On the passenger seat sat the guitar I'd picked up this morning as an anniversary gift for Bryan—our twenty-eighth. The guitar was a statement. Occasionally, he bemoaned the fact he'd never learned to play an instrument. Knowing him as long as I had, I knew he'd never give that dream wings. A true miser, parting with a dollar was painful to him. Financial security was important to me, too, but to me, his mindset was extreme and had become a bone of contention between us, especially after I'd spent my grandmother's inheritance leasing and renovating Break Thyme.

We could afford indulgences, but we rarely indulged. With the guitar and twelve lessons, I hoped to spark enough joy in Bryan to help him see the value in pursuing dreams. Sure, strumming a guitar wasn't as risky a venture as opening a café. The point I wanted to make was that dreams made life worth living and by pursuing them, we were setting a good example for our kids.

I wanted to get home before he did so I could hide the guitar, and it was almost four-thirty now. How did it get so late? Whatever Bryan had to discuss, we were going to do it over a home-cooked dinner, another reason I had to get moving.

Later, by the time my husband came home, I was sure the woman in the park was no different from the lowlife who'd scammed my mother's friends. Bryan would probably find Beverly's story amusing.

I turned down the heat under the stir-fry and greeted Bryan as he came into the kitchen. For a second, I wanted to say more than just hello but seeing him brought back the sting of the argument we'd had that morning when he'd promised to do me a favor and not say I told you so when my café failed. I was so tired of the tension between us and constantly prayed Break Thyme would be a marvelous success, so maybe he'd begin to support my dream.

"Hello," he said. "Did you have a good day?" His demeanor was as cool as mine.

Should I tell him about my mother or Beverly first?

I let out a slow breath, and for a second I tried to see Bryan through the eyes of another woman, a woman like Beverly the bombshell. Despite a slight sag in his jowls and a receding salt-and-pepper hairline, he was still a good-looking man. The way he carried himself, he had swagger. I'd always thought him sexy.

"You won't believe what happened to my mother today," I said. Our son had been in touch with his grandmother, so I was leaving whatever needed to happen next to fix her email in his hands.

Bryan usually headed for the mail, but he just stood there, gaze glued to his phone before looking up. "I heard. Jordan told me." He set his cell on the counter. "It's too bad. You'd think everyone would know by now these requests for money aren't legit."

"Apparently not. So far, the hobnocking thieves are up four hundred bucks."

He didn't crack a smile at *hobnocking*. "Jordan is trying to get her contact list back." He came close enough to peer in the cast iron pan. I sensed tension, but that wasn't a surprise. Sadly, I was getting used to the disquiet between us, the choosing of just the right words to keep him abreast of the café progression, but not set him off on his rants about my foolish ideas and how they'd put us in the poorhouse.

"I hope he can help," I said. "I made a shrimp stir-fry for dinner. Obviously." I hoped the small talk would help to patch over the insensitive things we'd flung at each other earlier, even though his words, repeated too often, still stung.

Nearly three-quarters of new coffee shops fail in their first five years, you know.

That dismal fact was a slight exaggeration and yes, of course, I knew that. I'd done my homework every step of the way—research, business planning, financials, permits, layout, sourcing, and purchasing—to name a few of the points I'd covered. One step at a time, I'd told myself.

Location was everything, which was why I'd waited for a lakefront property. Along with gourmet coffee, I'd offer boutique, artisan drinks and treats from our local bakery. Henrietta made the best almond croissants in the Milky Way. My plan to infuse herbs and spices into the menu would make Break Thyme distinct and memorable.

Atmosphere was one of the most important contributors to success. So, it made sense to expand into the space offered by the bicycle shop next door for the room I called the Cozy Nook, a place for customers to linger, relax, and chat or read. Plus, I'd gotten the space for a steal.

I pulled my thoughts from their merry-go-round and lifted the lid from the pot of rice. Cooked. This was as good a time as any to tell him about the woman from the park. I moved the pot off the heat. "Remember that associate of yours who died a couple of months ago in a car accident?"

"Yeah." He took a step back and squeezed his eyes shut for a second. "Listen, I need to talk to you about something. It's serious."

I bristled at his ignoring what I had to say and tried to imagine a way his lead-in could turn out well. It's serious—because we won the lottery? It's serious—because I realized I should support you and help you succeed? It's serious—because I've never loved you more than I do right now?

I shut off the stove and turned to face him. His grim expression made my chest tighten.

"This is related to Jim's death." Bryan jabbed his hand through his hair leaving a chunk sticking straight up. Under other circumstances, I'd be grinning.

"I met a woman at the funeral," he said.

Any inkling of humor was sucked out of the room with those words. *I met a woman.* Beverly?

"She's...she was...she wanted some help setting up a trust. She came into the bank to discuss the details." His gaze flicked to me, then down to his shoes. After all these years, he could never leave those shoes on the doormat like I asked.

I swallowed and crushed my molars together to keep myself focused and not have me obsessing over trivial things like shoes.

He cleared his throat. "I didn't realize it at the time, but she didn't call me just to set up a trust. It was a cover to set me up. And I fell for it, Quinn. I'm sorry."

So the problem was a professional one? "Fell for it? What does that mean?"

His expression hardened. "Things haven't exactly been warm between us lately."

I sure hoped he wasn't insinuating that was my fault. I'd gently explained how my libido worked. How it was impossible for me to feel turned on by someone who'd turned against me. And it was beyond me what our love life had to do with a setup. "That's because, in front of our kids and our friends, you *pretended* to support my café, but when we're alone you're sullen and you've been nasty since I signed the lease." I was repeating myself and could have said more, but we'd already had that argument to no satisfactory end. "Just tell me what happened."

"I crossed a line. Things got physical."

Physical? Bile rose in my throat. So far, I'd not let my mind go there. Honestly, I'd not thought Bryan capable of sexual deceit. Did every wife think that way? Or just the naïve ones? I should have noticed the signs. What were the signs? We'd drifted apart. Yes, that had to be one. When he worked late, I was okay with it. I didn't miss him. I'd wanted a break from the constant criticisms. That now seemed like a pretty big sign.

"I didn't have ... intercourse," he said, pulling out a chair, pushing it back in. "It didn't go that far."

That far? How far was not *that far?* He'd wanted to have sex, but was interrupted? *Don't picture it. That far* wasn't the kind of thing you should admit to your spouse unless you wanted to break her into pieces.

He crossed his arms in front of him. Something was missing. No damp eyes. No head held in shame. No move to touch me. I'd been married to him a long time. I knew him. I knew when he was sorry. This wasn't sorry. This was worried. There was something else.

"Was her name Beverly Foster?" I said, the words scorching my throat.

His eyes flew open, giving me some satisfaction. *Ha. I'm not as ignorant as you think.* "How do you know that?" he asked.

"You better tell me what happened," I repeated. He wasn't going to leave me hanging. If anyone was left hanging, it was going to be him. Not me. I wasn't the one stopping short of intercourse.

"The police questioned me today."

What? A hollow echo filled my ears. I hadn't been expecting that. Not police. Nothing to do with police. "What for?"

He tugged at the button at the bottom of his shirt. *Yeah, you better squirm, mister.* "How do you know about Beverly?" he asked.

My fingers clenched around the wooden spoon in my hand. I hadn't realized I was holding it. "She spoke to me in the park today. What did the police want?"

His gaze was sharp now, piercing me. "No, she didn't. That's impossible. What's wrong with you?"

"What's wrong with me? How dare you speak to me like I don't know who I talked to just hours ago." The anger coursing through me felt good, better than shock. He was the one in the wrong here. He had no right to tell me what I'd seen was impossible. I was sick of him treating me like I was an uninformed imbecile who needed his help to make every decision. "This woman followed me. She said her name was Beverly Foster. How many Beverly Fosters did you meet at Jim's funeral and nearly have sex with?"

His eyes showed a flicker of guilt. Just a flicker. "Beverly Foster is dead," he said. "She was killed two days ago."

Chapter Three

I DIDN'T KNOW WHAT Bryan was trying to pull on me, but I knew what I'd seen—who I'd seen. I'd had a conversation with the woman for crying out loud. She'd introduced herself.

"She's not dead," I countered. "She can't have been killed. I spoke with her this morning, and she had a lot to say for a dead person." We weren't living in a horror movie. Just because she'd been as pale as a ghost didn't mean she was...a ghost. I shivered and hugged myself, recoiling from the idea. "What are you suggesting, Bryan? How did I know her name if she didn't talk to me?"

He just stared at me, like he couldn't figure out what I was up to. It looked good on him. "I've just come from the sheriff's office," he said glumly. "Someone shot Beverly Foster in the back on Saturday night."

No. That made no sense, so just for a moment, I set that impossibility aside. My brain didn't know what to do with it and the stress, I believed, was making it hard to comprehend more than one shocking disclosure at a time. "Wait a minute. Why did the sheriff question you?"

His knuckles went white in his clenched fist. "They found my name in her phone. I was the last person she called—on Friday afternoon."

I felt like throwing up. "Do they think you killed her?"

"For God's sake. Do you think I could kill someone? I was with you on Saturday night, Quinn."

"I didn't say I thought you killed anyone. And it doesn't matter what I think—apparently. I see what's happening here, Bryan. You told me about this thing with Beverly—not to come clean or ask for forgiveness—but because you need me as an alibi."

He met my eyes, matter of fact, as if he'd done nothing wrong. "We were home together all night. I'm just asking you to tell the truth."

Scumbag!

I became aware of the crumbling sound of our marriage disintegrating. I let out my breath and shook my head. I would not make this easy for him. I'd seen the bombshell he got physical with. Is she what he wanted? After nearly three decades together, my husband didn't want guitar lessons. He wanted to strum a blonde.

"And, Quinn, don't tell the sheriff you've been speaking to a dead woman."

Or an imposter. "Get out, Bryan. You can find somewhere else to sleep."

"Fine." He looked relieved to go. He picked up his cell phone and went downstairs to our bedroom to pack a bag, I assumed.

"Don't come back!" I slumped into the chair he'd pulled out. Laid my forehead on the table. And cried.

Instead of stir-fry, I had gin for dinner. In my pajamas. I was a lightweight when it came to alcohol and usually stopped after two drinks, another by-product of careening down the hill toward my golden years.

After my third gin and tonic, I'd finished ranting.

I wasn't sure where the greater insult fell—the affair or the accusation that I'd lied about meeting Beverly. Me, the liar? Oh, the gall. Who'd been keeping secrets about getting physical? Not me. Him! He was a scumbag, all right!

Okay, maybe I wasn't finished ranting.

And, on the subject of dishonesty, I wasn't buying the no-sex part. His comment about no intercourse was smoke and mirrors. Irrelevant. Sex wasn't just inter—

I didn't want to think about it.

Yet I kept coming back to the conversation I'd had in the park. I hadn't imagined the woman calling herself Beverly Foster. She'd mentioned the funeral. I might have a buzz going on at the moment, but I'd been lucid until my liquid dinner.

I brought my laptop and the bottle of gin into the living room. If Beverly Foster was shot in the back two days ago, there'd be a news story. I'd been so busy over the last few days—sourcing the finest guitar for my cheating husband—that I'd not read the news.

The first thing I did was type Beverly Foster into the search bar. There it was—*Woman Shot Dead Outside*

Swingers' Club. Seriously? A swingers' club? In Bookend Bay? I was so out of touch—which was fine with me. Had Bryan been to this club? Was that how his relationship with Beverly started? Did she introduce him to it, so he could play out his secret—

Stop! It did no good to spiral into imagined scenarios. I needed to keep to the facts.

I read the article. Turned out the club wasn't in town, but well on the outskirts. Beverly Foster's body was found in a garden. As Bryan said, she'd been shot in the back on Saturday night, found Sunday morning by a pedestrian walking his dog—it was always a dog-walker or a jogger. I kept scrolling and finally reached what I was looking for. A photo.

Shoot. Was that my doorbell? Didn't it just figure company came calling when I was drinking alone? I didn't have to answer, although my truck was in the driveway, so whoever it was would presume I was home.

Crossing the living room to the window, I peeked out toward the front door. A police officer was standing at attention on my stone walkway.

Cripes. The police! She turned, squinted slightly, then waved at me. Darn observational skills.

I sighed, looking down at my pink pajamas with *I Sparkle in the Mornings* splashed across the front in silver glitter. As I opened the door, I ran my tongue across my teeth, as if I could wipe away the smell of gin.

"Quinn Delaney?" she asked after I said hello.

I admitted that was true.

"I'm Officer Birke. Can I come in? I'd like to ask you a few questions."

Why had I not thought ahead before getting boozed up? Bryan said the police wanted me to verify his alibi. I guess I'd been expecting a phone call. Were they purposely trying to catch me unawares?

"Yes. Come in." I stood back while she entered, then closed the door.

The officer was stalky with a ruddy complexion, hair pulled back in a bun. She looked a lot tougher than me and less sparkly.

"Would you like to sit down?" As soon as I said it, I saw the bottle of gin in the middle of my coffee table.

"Sure." She chose one of the armchairs opposite the couch. Her gaze drifted over the bottle to meet mine.

"I don't usually have liquor bottles so close at hand," I said, as though I'd done something wrong. "It's not every day my husband admits his contact information was found on a murdered woman's phone."

She may not have been expecting my candor, but I wanted to get through this as fast as possible, and I didn't want her pussyfooting around my husband's involvement with this investigation or case or whatever.

"I understand," she said, referencing the gin I imagined. "Is Mr. Delaney home?"

"No. He is not."

She looked over to the floor beside the couch. Her eyes widened. "Whoa. That is one big cat."

I followed her gaze to see Oreo, my Maine Coon stalking into the room. Officer Birke's reaction was typical of people unfamiliar with the breed. Oreo was the size of a small lynx, black-faced, white-chested, with tufts on his ears. He looked at her and gurgled—at least that's what I called the sound he made regularly.

"He's a Maine Coon. Come here, Oreo," I tapped the seat cushion beside me, and he bounced up.

"That is the coolest cat I've ever seen." Her gaze moved from Oreo to me. "I asked the sheriff if I could come by to verify your husband's alibi. I thought it might be more discreet to get your statement here. Save you the trouble of coming into the station."

Because gossip spread like wildfire in this town? Or because she wanted to check on the veracity of my character? Ha! *Not sure how reliable that witness is, Sheriff. She was well in her cups.* Oops, sorry, Bryan.

"Your husband said he was with you all of Saturday night. Can you corroborate this?"

A part of me wanted to lace my response with uncertainty, but that was the wounded part. Ultimately, I'd protect Bryan to protect my kids. I couldn't imagine what it would be like for them to have their father accused of murder. "Yes, I can. We were home together from six o'clock Saturday night until about ten a.m. on Sunday. He didn't leave the house."

"You're sure he couldn't have slipped out while you were sleeping?"

"It's unlikely. I typically wake up a couple of times in the night." And Bryan could thank my middle-aged bladder for that. "I would have noticed if he was missing."

She looked skeptical and made a note in her book.

Wait. Saturday night. Was that when I'd found him in his office in the middle of the night? He rarely got up through the night. Or had that been Friday? What day was today? Oh gosh, I couldn't think. Break Thyme's sign was going to be hung on Monday. Seemed like days ago. So today was still Monday. That meant Saturday was two nights ago. That seemed right. Okay, so what time had I found him downstairs?

"Er, what time was the woman killed?"

"Estimated time of death is between twelve a.m. and three a.m." She paused and leaned forward. "Do you have something to add? Take your time, Mrs. Delaney."

I tried to remember if I'd looked at the clock that night, but the memory wasn't there. I had no idea what time Bryan had been downstairs. Because he was awake, was it more likely he'd left the house at some point? He'd said he couldn't sleep and decided to get some work done. I often used the bathroom around four a.m., but I couldn't be sure of the time. Should I tell the police officer and cast doubt on my husband? He had been home, so my answer wouldn't change. "I just remembered that I did wake up and he was home, also awake, but I don't know what time that was."

"Okay." Officer Birke's hands were clasped, resting on a knee. "Did you suspect your husband was having an affair with Beverly Foster?"

Why was she asking me that? Cripes! The wife would be a suspect in a case like this, wouldn't she? "No. No, I didn't. I'd never heard of her until today." I paused, feeling myself grow warm, but I didn't dare lift the hair from my brow. Darn hot flashes! I didn't want an officer trained in the art of putting two and two together to think I was sweating because I wasn't telling the truth.

My self-preservation instincts were on full alert, but my brain was stymied from the gin. My tongue felt thick. I needed to think. Should I mention the Beverly impostor I'd spoken to that afternoon?

I will give you the evidence you'll need to absolve your husband. How would I explain that meeting without sounding crazy? Did it sound crazy? She'd introduced herself as Beverly Foster. I couldn't think straight with the officer staring at me. I glanced at my laptop. I needed to see the picture of Beverly. I needed to know if the woman I met looked anything like the dead person. *Pull yourself together!*

"Bryan told me about Beverly Foster just tonight, hence the gin," I added, my voice cracking on the last words. "I'm sorry. I'm quite upset by all of this. It's so fresh. I've had no time to process it."

"I understand. Thank you, Ms. Delaney. Are you going to be okay?"

"Yes. I'm going to bed soon." I nodded my head toward the gin. "I wasn't planning on drinking the whole bottle."

She made a soft sound, almost a tsk. "Is there someone who could come and stay with you?"

"Yes," I said, thinking of my friend Toni, but she was out of town until tomorrow. "I just want to be alone right now."

Officer Birke nodded. "I know what it's like to be blind-sided. At least you know the truth now."

I supposed that was one way of looking at things, but did I know the truth? Maybe some of it, but my conversation with an alleged murdered woman left more questions than answers. Officer Birke was right though, I'd never get past this if I didn't know the truth.

I walked her to the door, glad she was leaving.

"Thank you for your cooperation," she said. "You take care, now."

"You, too."

After I shut the door, I realized I was trembling. I took a deep breath and looked at myself in the mirror. My puffy eyes still showed signs of the emotional overflow that prompted the gin. My bangs had curled from perspiration. I looked haggard, and it was all Bryan's fault. Not just the affair. He'd made me a suspect in a murder. A murder! I'd be a fool to think otherwise. Officer Birke may have acted compassionately, yet she could also think I was a jealous spouse who'd killed her husband's lover in a fit of rage.

And another thing. I hadn't told the truth to that officer about the woman in the park. Why? Because Bryan had made me believe the police would think I was crazy. He'd actually told me not to tell them, and I'd listened. He'd planted seeds of doubt like he always did. Undermining my confidence. Making me second guess myself.

Why? Why did he constantly do this? Why hadn't he asked me about the woman I'd met? Was he hiding something other than an affair?

If he thought I wasn't going to dig until I got to the truth, he didn't know me very well. This seemed to be the new theme of our marriage because I sure didn't know him as well as I'd thought. And I wasn't positive Bryan hadn't left the house Saturday night, yet I'd given him an alibi. Although whether I'd provided a reliable alibi, I couldn't be sure. If the police suspected me of murdering his mistress, I supposed he and I were each other's alibis. How reliable was that?

I hugged myself tight, anger and hurt welling in my chest, as another ugly realization dawned.

I didn't trust my husband.

We were no longer a team. He hadn't been broken up over his affair—not like he should have been if he cared about me and our marriage. He'd not begged for forgiveness. He'd not said he loved me and wanted to fix this.

I couldn't imagine him being capable of murder, but the chill creeping up my spine told me something was terribly wrong. The urge to protect myself was overwhelming and to know exactly what the woman in the park wanted and what evidence she had to absolve Bryan.

Before Officer Birke arrived, I'd been looking for proof that I hadn't had a conversation with a dead person, and I'd just found a photo of the victim.

Chapter Four

THE PHOTO OF BEVERLY Foster wasn't of great quality, but it was good enough to confirm the unsmiling blonde in the picture was the same woman I'd met that morning. I remembered the mole under her eye.

But how could that be?

I thought back to my observations of Beverly—she'd looked cadaverously pale, and she'd disappeared into thin air, but she couldn't have been murdered on Saturday night if I'd seen her on Monday afternoon. Okay, so what was the reasonable explanation for there being two identical Beverly Fosters, one who was murdered and one who approached me pretending to be the murdered woman?

Maybe Beverly Foster had an identical twin and unimaginative parents who named both girls Beverly. I thought about that for a minute and decided it wasn't likely.

Maybe the twin assumed Beverly's name after she died. But what was the advantage of that?

I thought about it for another couple of minutes and came up blank. Who was the woman I'd met in the park and why was she playing games with me?

Come on, think through the brain fog. Sober up!

The stress of all this was putting me on the edge of a tension headache. And no wonder. I'd had a horrible day. The point of the gin was to put me in a buzzy place where reality was nicely blurred. Maybe I was pushing myself too hard. Perhaps sobering up wasn't a good idea quite yet.

Still, I'd better keep hydrated. I set my laptop aside and went into the kitchen for something to eat and a glass of water.

Oreo padded along after me and stopped at his empty food bowl. Meowing, he wound himself between my calves.

"Yes, sir, right away." I leaned down to give his head a scratch, then retrieved a tin of food from the cupboard. He followed behind, yowling and rubbing against my leg. "I'm moving as fast as I can, buddy. If you trip me, neither of us will be eating." I opened the tin, scooped half into his bowl, covered the tin, and put it in the refrigerator.

With Oreo happily munching, I spooned stir-fry onto a plate and put away the rest. While eating, I leafed through a culinary magazine and tried to clear my mind.

After an hour or so, I felt slightly better. My head wasn't buzzy any longer, and I'd started to think about Beverly Foster again.

Back on the sofa, I woke up my computer to see what else the Internet had to say about her. A search generated images of women with the same name, but none were the bombshell I'd met. I scrolled through pages of Beverly Foster listings; too many to determine which, if any of these women, had been getting physical with Bryan.

Fingers on the keyboard, I thought about how to narrow things down. An idea came to me. What if I did a reverse image search to see if I could find pictures that matched Beverly's photo? First, I searched for instructions on how to do this.

Back to the news article, I clicked on the photo of Beverly and saved it on my desktop. Following instructions, I searched the Internet for the photo. A selection of visually similar images appeared, but upon close inspection there were no matches. No mole.

On the third page, I found a good match; at least I was pretty sure it was her. The photo was of a man and a woman. She had a mole under her eye but looked like a younger Beverly. The man, holding a circular saw, stood beside Beverly in front of a dilapidated house above the headline Hill Construction House Flippers Bring Hoarder's House Back to Life. The site belonged to a home renovation blogger. I read the article, but it didn't identify the woman.

I looked up Hill Construction and found their website. It was owned by Andrew Hill. I scrolled through the site but saw no mention of Beverly. Using the camera on my phone, I snapped a photo of Beverly and the man with the saw, then bookmarked both websites.

The woman in the park demanded I find Hannah Wyatt, so I googled Hannah next. Like Beverly, there were many people named Hannah Wyatt. I looked at a few listings but saw nothing that tied to Beverly Foster.

I searched for Hannah Wyatt and Beverly Foster together. Nothing. Beverly Foster and Hill Construction. Nothing. Hannah Wyatt and Hill Construction. Nothing.

I threw up my hands in defeat.

Why couldn't the woman I'd met in the park find Hannah Wyatt herself? Why ask me, the wife of the man she was getting physical with? None of this made any sense, and I was getting nowhere.

Would that woman, whoever she was, approach me again? A shiver shook my spine. Did I want another encounter with the Beverly Foster impersonator? Not really, but how else would I get answers?

I couldn't stand the thought of asking my condescending, cheating, untrustworthy husband what he knew about Beverly. He'd made it clear he didn't believe I'd spoken to her. And, considering she no longer had a pulse, I couldn't argue that without sounding unhinged.

I stared at my computer screen, but I wasn't taking anything in. Stressed out, I needed time for the shock to wear off before I could think clearly.

Did I want answers?

I didn't have to think for long. Of course, I did. I always did. My brother once said I was most alive when the things in my life were uncertain. My mother had corroborated this by saying if someone were to look at my genetic material under a microscope, they'd see a double dose of curiosity genes.

Thump! My cat jumped up on the arm of the sofa, giving me a start.

"Some warning would be nice, Oreo." He cocked his black head, then stepped onto my keyboard and sprawled across my lap, leaning his head against my chest, looking up at me.

"You should think twice before scaring me half to death. If I drop dead, you'll be here alone with an empty food bowl." I gave his head a scratch as he rubbed his cheek against my wrist. Despite his putting an end to my Internet search, I was grateful for his presence and the soothing sound of his purring.

By the time he was snoring beside me, I'd made a decision. I woke up my computer, found Hill Construction's address, and typed it into my phone for the next morning. Since they were in a photo together, Andrew Hill must know the name of this woman and might know if she had a look-alike.

If the police were sizing me up as a suspect in Beverly's murder, I couldn't leave my fate to chance. Whatever it took, I had to keep digging until I discovered the true identity of the woman in the park, how she knew Bryan was involved with a murdered woman, and what evidence she was holding back that could absolve him because Bryan couldn't have killed somebody.

Could he? No, not the man I knew.

My mouth went dry. Bryan had never gotten up in the middle of the night to work—not once that I could remember, yet he'd been downstairs very much awake the night Beverly was murdered.

Of course, that didn't mean he'd been out of the house and with her that night.

A knot tightened in my stomach as a devastating realization took hold of me. How did I know he hadn't been with her? I hadn't even known there was a *her*. I couldn't be certain of anything when it came to him anymore.

And his phone number had been the last one she'd called.

Chapter Five

THE NEXT MORNING, I stood in the kitchen, staring out the window, but nothing outside was registering. My mind seemed to have hijacked my ability to prioritize routine stuff like breakfast and planning my day. I supposed an inability to focus was normal, considering the day I'd had yesterday.

Bryan hadn't come home, which was fine with me. I was still fuming and feeling an absurd satisfaction that his lover had shown up dead. I wasn't proud of that thought, but it was stuck in my head none-the-less.

With my phone in hand, I sat on the window seat in the kitchen beside Oreo and called my friend Toni. She'd just gotten home from her daughter's place in Marquette.

I'd planned to wait until we met in person to tell her about the murder of Bryan's mistress and the Beverly look-alike in the park, but it all came spewing out.

The thirty-minute conversation that followed had me feeling grounded and even stronger by the time I hung up. Friends for nearly thirty years, I could be completely honest with Toni, and I could count on her for intelligent, honest, loving advice.

We'd planned to meet in an hour to do what we could to unravel the Beverly mystery. With my best friend's infallible support, I was going to get through this. I wasn't overwhelmed any longer because I wasn't alone in this.

Oreo was snoring beside me. I eased off the seat, trying not to disturb him and heard my front door open.

My heart jumped into my throat. *Don't let it be Bryan.*

"Hey, Mom!" came from the foyer. By the sounds of the chatter, there was a crowd at the door. Oh no. I wasn't ready to talk about any of this to my kids. I couldn't imagine ever telling them the horrible story about their father's murdered mistress, especially with the added absurdity of imposter Beverly's demand. If we had to tell the kids, it was something Bryan and I would eventually have to tackle together.

Anger burbled up inside me at the dreadful position he'd put me in. I tamped it down, plastered a smile on my face, and headed to the front entrance to find my two kids plus one.

"Hello, my loves," I said, feeling a small fraction of cheer at their smiling faces. "What a pleasant surprise."

Samantha, my twenty-five-year-old, had her light brown hair pulled back in a tail that swung as she bounded into my arms for a hug. "Seriously? You invited us for breakfast," she pointed out.

Shoot! I remembered now. I'd invited the kids over to celebrate Samantha having finished her degree in Entrepreneurship Management. We'd have a more substantial celebration after her commencement.

"Of course, I remembered that." I set my gaze on my son Jordan's new girlfriend. "I meant it's a surprise to see Chelsea. I wasn't expecting you to join us. How nice." I gave my son Jordan a hug and then Chelsea.

"Hello," she said, going stiff under my embrace. Not a hugger, but she sure smelled fragrant. Like expensive perfume. For my sensitive tummy, it was too much. I stepped back.

Jordan was dressed casually, in sweats. He scooped up his long sandy-blonde hair and tied it back in a tail like his sister's. "Chelsea was free, so I asked her to join us. That's okay, right?"

"Yes, of course. Come in. It's nice to see you again, Chelsea."

She made a sound of agreement—I think. It wasn't yet 9 a.m. and she looked stunning. I didn't know how she got her hair to shine like that, and the waves looked like a work of art. Similar to Beverly's, I thought, then balked, pushing that comparison from my thoughts.

"Did you speak to your grandmother, Jordan?" I questioned, pleased to have remembered my mother's crisis.

"A couple of times. It sucks, but at least Gramma and her friends are aware of these scams now. I got her a new email address and sent her some links, so she can read up on these things."

"Can you send those links to me, too?" I asked. It seemed like every week, I received a phone call threatening doom if I didn't give them personal information, or a couple thousand dollars to release the millions being held in my name. Jordan had told me to never answer an online quiz or survey and to avoid mystery shopper jobs or work from home ads. These prospects didn't entice me, but it was a good bet someone out there was clicking on these fraudulent opportunities.

I turned to my daughter. "Sam, can you put on a pot of coffee, please?"

We all went into the kitchen. Jordan detoured to the window seat to say hello to Oreo.

I may have forgotten about breakfast, but thankfully, I'd shopped for it. I planned to make mimosas but hadn't chilled the champagne. My minor hangover called for something greasy, but I was going to serve bagels and lox. I certainly wasn't craving more alcohol, but I wanted to toast Sam's achievement.

Chelsea sat down at the table while Samantha started the coffee.

"What can I do to help?" Jordan asked.

"Can you please grab the bottle of champagne from the pantry and put it in the fridge?" I looked over at Chelsea, who was admiring her fingernails—each one a different color. "Oh my gosh, you've got running shoes painted on your fingernails," I said. "That's cute!"

She smiled. "I know. The spa does them. You should check them out."

"Maybe I will for my café opening. A coffee cup painted on each finger or maybe a sprig of thyme."

Samantha laughed. "Mom, you should totally do that. I was hoping for scones this morning, but I smell nothing baking. What are we having?"

I gave her an apologetic look and rhymed off our menu. "Bagels are in the bread drawer if you wouldn't mind getting them toasted. I'll get the rest." I made a list in my head: salmon, cream cheese, red onion, lemon, and capers. Text Toni to tell her I may run late.

"There's no champagne in here," Jordan said, standing just inside the walk-in pantry.

I rolled my eyes because I knew the bottle was on the shelf on the right side. What was it with men not being able to find things? "You have to move your head from side to side," I parroted the advice I'd been giving him for nearly twenty-seven years.

I opened the fridge and leaned in to get the package of smoked salmon. On the lower shelf sat a serving platter covered in plastic wrap. I didn't remember putting it there.

Next to the platter was a nicely chilled bottle of champagne.

"Never mind, Jordan. It's already in the fridge."

"Uh-huh," Jordan said in a righteous tone. "Mom, do you know what year it is?"

"Never mind the dementia jokes. I'm too young," I said, while secretly losing confidence in my razor-sharp mind as I pulled out the platter. Everything we needed for our breakfast was beautifully laid out. Capers in a pinch bowl, cream cheese in a matching black and white dipping bowl, lemon, onion, cucumber slices, salmon, and sprigs of dill. I tried, but I couldn't remember putting this platter together. Of course, the memory loss was stress related. Stress always wreaked havoc on my memory, and yesterday had been a doozy.

"Dad probably chilled the champagne," Samantha said. "Where is he?'

Had Bryan put together this platter? He was an excellent cook, but I couldn't imagine when he would have done this. I realized I was hesitating when I looked up and saw the three of them staring at me.

"Uh, he had some kind of emergency and had to go into work early." It came out sounding like a lie, but the kids didn't seem to notice.

We had a nice breakfast and a toast to Samantha's graduation. I tried to engage Chelsea in conversation, asking about her acting prospects, but she offered the barest minimum. I didn't push it. The first and last time we'd met; I'd asked if she was planning to move to a big city—surely Bookend Bay was no hive of acting opportunities. I'd been surprised to learn she had no plans to move in the works.

"Chelsea's putting together a portfolio," Jordan said. "She's going to need an agent. I think she could work as a model. She's got the right look."

"I could see myself on a billboard," Chelsea said.

Samantha and I exchanged glances. "I'd rather die, but that'd be exciting for you," Samantha said.

I reached across the table to stack Chelsea's plate onto mine. "I'm sorry, guys, but I've got to get going."

"How many days, Mom?" Samantha asked.

For the first time in months, I hadn't woken with my café opening on my mind. "It must be twenty-three days now."

My kids and I cleaned up the kitchen. Chelsea didn't move, at least not until Oreo leaped up onto her lap. She let out a cry. As she stood, Oreo thumped to the ground and looked back at her with an evil eye.

"Ugh, cat hair," she said, brushing away the hair or two that might have stuck. "These jeans are Leilas."

I'd never heard of that brand. I looked at Jordan to see how he was taking this disdain of his beloved cat.

"Sorry about that," he apologized. "I'll get you a lint roller."

Samantha and I exchanged another look. Okay, it wasn't just me thinking Chelsea was a bit of a princess. I wondered about Jordan's attraction to this young woman, other than that she was quite pretty.

I'd recently read an article about how some men liked to feel needed. Jordan was a natural caregiver. Looking after a woman might make him feel manly, possibly like a hero. I understood this, but I also understood how tiring his life could become with a woman like this. My brother's ex-wife had been a handful.

I stopped myself right there. It wasn't fair to make assumptions about Chelsea and Jordan's relationship. They were both adults. Since I hardly knew Chelsea, I vowed to make an effort to focus on her good qualities. As soon as they became obvious.

In the meantime, I had my own relationship concerns. I needed to look after myself right now. I intended to do what I could to protect myself from being considered a suspect in Beverly Foster's murder, and after talking to Toni, I had a pretty good idea where to start.

Chapter Six

I DROVE TO THE community of Beach Meadows, a ten-minute drive from Bookend Bay, to pick up Toni. After being waved through the gate, I crossed over the small bridge between two fountained ponds edged in ornamental grasses and blooming daffodils. Gardens in this neighborhood were a point of pride. In a couple of weeks, when there was no chance of frost, everyone would be out planting their annuals.

Widowed eleven years ago, Toni had moved into a modular home in this charming, lakeside community. Having downsized considerably, she loved her simpler life.

When I arrived, Toni was sitting outside on her porch. She hurried down the stairs to the passenger side of my truck. A colorful hairband she'd bought in Mexico tucked her blonde hair off her forehead. I'd bought a hairband, too, but then didn't think it suited me to have my bangs off my face. I made a mental note to give mine to Toni.

Inside the truck, she leaned across the console and hugged me. "I'm so sorry, my friend. How are you?"

"Well, night sweats are no longer my greatest malady, but I'll be okay."

"I know you will." Toni sat back in her seat and reached for the belt. "The nice thing about reaching the age of internal heat waves is that we've learned life doesn't always turn out as planned. We've survived all the twists and turns and ups and downs, and we'll keep on surviving. You didn't make your happiness contingent on Bryan—you never did. So, you'll get past this crappy moment and get your happiness back."

She was right. We were resilient. We believed in viewing life's challenges realistically and taking whatever steps we had to take to surpass difficult situations and end up happy. Eventually. I wasn't there yet.

Toni reached into her purse, then tossed me a treat wrapped in pink foil. "It's artisan chocolate, and I've got a dozen. Gotta keep up our energy."

"Chocolate is the best. And you are, too. Thanks, Toni."

She unwrapped her piece. "Now, I've got a few more things to say."

I let out my breath.

"When you told me about Bryan's affair, I was shocked, so I can only imagine how his betrayal felt to you. Bryan's not perfect, not by a long shot, but I thought he had more integrity than that."

"I agree. He didn't call it an affair, which is a copout. It's his lame attempt to believe he's still reputable."

She scoffed. "You know, Quinn, I wasn't going to say anything..."

"Say anything about what?"

"You know I care about you."

"Yes, I know that," I said cautiously.

"And that's why I'm going to stick my nose in...furt her. I don't like the way Bryan has been treating you. He's become critical of you. I thought it was because he was insecure and felt threatened, as if your success will somehow demean him. But now I think it's possible he became overly critical of you to justify his carrying on with another woman."

It was uncomfortable to hear Toni talk about my marriage, but I knew she was being honest and her take on the situation made me feel marginally better. I looked away, checked the mirrors, and reversed out of the driveway. "That actually makes sense, now that I think about it." I thought back to Jim's funeral and realized Bryan had met Beverly before I'd signed the lease for Break Thyme. "He's had nothing good to say about Break Thyme since I signed the lease. We had a brutal argument yesterday morning. He said I'm going to fail and lose my investment. He won't give my café a sliver of optimism." My neck muscles were growing tense. When I stopped at the end of the road to turn onto the highway, I turned my head from side to side to give my neck a stretch.

Another thing about reaching my late forties was I now had decades of self-introspection behind me. I knew the fear of failure was a trigger for me, so I'd chosen to use Bryan's negativity to spur me on to success, but it wasn't as if I was fully immune to his opinions. Lately, I had to constantly bolster myself.

Toni scoffed. "You're the last person I'd expect to fail at anything. I don't know anyone who works harder than you do, Quinn. The whole town is looking forward to your opening, and I'm here to help, and I know your kids are, too. Don't you ever stop believing that Break Thyme is going to be a roaring success."

I expelled an angst-filled breath and felt better. "I needed that. Thank you. I don't know how people survive without girlfriends." I was going to get through this thing with Bryan and be okay—better than okay. His absence was a blessing. With my wits, ambition, life experience, good friends and family, I had everything I needed to see things clearly. To tackle the murdered mistress dilemma and triumph!

"You've always been there for me," Toni said. "So, where are we going?"

I glanced at her and realized I had no idea. Okay, so maybe I wasn't quite the guru of fortitude yet. "That would be a good thing to know, wouldn't it?" I pulled the truck off onto the shoulder.

Toni smiled and nodded. "I always find information like that helpful."

When I'd spilled my guts earlier that morning, we'd decided to pay Andrew Hill a visit and see what he knew about Beverly Foster. "Hill Construction's address is on my phone. I just have to get directions."

Toni handed me my purse. "Are you going to tell Andrew Hill you had a conversation with his dearly departed employee?"

I smiled. "Might not start with that, but hopefully he'll know something about Beverly's personal life."

"Like if she had a twin sister? Although that doesn't explain why the woman you met said she was Beverly."

I plugged in the address and got the directions. When I saw the route, I grimaced. "Shoot. I didn't notice his place is an hour and a half away," I said apologetically.

"You must have had something else on your mind," Toni said dryly.

"Yeah, a little something. I called them this morning and learned Andrew will be on site all day today. Should I just phone him instead of driving all that way?"

"I took the day off, so you're stuck with me all day." Toni worked at the schools and at the county hospital as a speech-language pathologist.

I turned to her and smiled. "I really appreciate that. Thank you."

"Any time. And I'm okay with a drive if you are. I think it will do you good to get out of town for an afternoon, no? And after, we can find a place to have dinner."

That actually sounded perfect to me. I didn't want to be at home. I handed Toni my phone. "Okay, then can you be our navigator?" My truck was manufactured before navigation systems were standard.

"Sure." She looked at the map. "Turn right at the next intersection.

I put the truck in drive, checked the mirrors, and pulled onto the road. "A Beverly twin would make me feel much better."

"Oh, I don't know," she said. "If you've been talking to a dead person, we get to have a sixth sense coming-out party."

I laughed. "Good point. We can invite a random phantom and a ghost from the coast."

"We should probably have a director specter, too."

"And a don't-fear-it spirit."

"Whatever happens, Quinn, don't give up the ghost."

Nothing like a good bout of silliness to dispel the horror of my last twenty-four hours. We listened to the comedy station as we drove, and I was remarkably rejuvenated by the time we arrived.

A mile off the highway, beside a gas station and grocery mart, sat a building with a bright yellow sign that said Hill Construction.

It was a chilly May morning, so I held my jacket closed as we walked to the front door. Inside, the showroom displayed a selection of cabinets, tile and counter samples, drawer pulls, as well as a full bathroom and kitchen. We waited for the receptionist to finish a phone call.

"I like this tile," Toni said, running her fingers across a display of blue and white patterned floor tiles.

"I like this marbled one," I said, noticing the receptionist had finished her call.

"Can I help you?" she asked as we approached.

"Yes. I called this morning. I'd like to speak to Andrew Hill."

She gave us a wide smile. "Sure. I'll get him for you."

Andrew Hill had the muscular build of a man who labored for a living. His striking ash- color hair was chin-length and tucked behind his ears. "Hello, I'm Andrew," he said, offering his hand. "What can I do for you?"

I shook his hand. "It's nice to meet you, Andrew. I'm Quinn Delaney and this is my friend Toni Miller. I'm wondering if you have a minute to help clear something up for us."

"I sure will try," he said. "Let's have a seat over here." We followed him to the showroom kitchen, where he pulled out two bar stools for Toni and me to sit at the island. I leaned against the white quartz.

"I don't know if you heard, but one of your previous employees may have died Saturday night," I said.

He blinked. "Really? Who died?"

"Beverly Foster."

His mouth twisted as he thought on it. "Hmm. Never heard of her."

Oh no. Had we really come all this way for nothing? I looked at Toni.

"Show him that picture of her you found," she said.

Oh, right. Of course. I pulled out my phone and found the snapshot I'd taken of Beverly and Andrew.

He took my phone and looked closely, then cocked his head. "She changed her last name. Used to be Gifford. Beverly's dead, huh?" He didn't look upset by the news.

"So, she did work with you about fifteen years ago?" I asked.

He gave a quick snort. "She worked with me all right. Beverly is my ex-wife, or was, I suppose."

"Oh!" said Toni. "That's a surprise."

A good surprise. He'd know about Beverly's siblings. It struck me as odd, though, that he showed not a sliver of sadness over the death of someone he must have loved.

"How'd she die?" he asked, still nonchalant.

"She was shot. In the back." I decided not to mention the swinger's club. He could learn those facts for himself if he wanted.

"Hmm. Well, I can't say I'm all that surprised."

That was a rather telling comment, I thought. Did that mean Beverly had an enemy or two that might draw the suspicion away from me?

"Not a lot of love lost between you two, huh?" said Toni.

Andrew shook his head. "Nope. It took me years to recover from that split. Beverly disappeared with over eighty-thousand dollars of our customer's deposits. I had to pay that money back. I was nearly ruined. My parents mortgaged their house for me."

"I'm sorry," I said. "That's pretty horrible." It did not surprise me to hear Beverly was of questionable moral character. It felt good to embrace my dislike of her.

"Yeah, well, it was a tough lesson and probably why I'm still single." He chuckled. "You have questions about Beverly? She didn't rip you off, did she?"

"No," I said, although it wasn't true. She'd ripped my husband out of our marriage. "I'm wondering about her family. Did she have siblings?"

"Yeah, she had an older sister."

Okay, good. This sister could be the woman I met. "Did they look alike?"

"Not really. At least I never thought they looked alike, but then again, I never met her. Beverly carried a photo of the two of them as kids. Denise was dark-haired and pudgier than Beverly, at that time anyway."

I sighed. So, her twin had not visited me.

"Any cousins who look like her?" Toni asked.

Andrew rubbed a smudge off the counter. "I don't know about that. She never mentioned cousins. All I knew was that she grew up in West Virginia, a place called Davisville—a real small-town—population no more than a thousand. She refused to talk about her childhood and had no plans to see her parents again. I figured they did a number on her."

I felt half an ounce of sympathy for the woman. It sounded like she'd had a rough upbringing.

Andrew was a good-looking man, but from the lines etched in his forehead and around his eyes, he appeared to be a decade or so older than Beverly.

"How old was Beverly?" I asked, realizing I'd missed that detail in her obituary.

He thought for a second. "I guess she would have been about forty-three."

"I would never have guessed that." She looked about thirty-five.

"She always said she didn't plan to age gracefully, although she sure loved those tanning beds. Still, at the first wrinkle, she would have had Botox injections, or a face-lift, or whatever women do nowadays."

I thought about the pale woman I'd met in the park. That woman was no sun-worshiper.

"Does that help you any?" he asked.

Not really. We were no closer to figuring out who the woman in the park was. "Yes, thank you. I appreciate your time."

"So, who was Beverly to you?" he asked, getting up and sliding his chair back under the counter.

He'd been forthcoming with us, so I decided to tell the truth. "She was having an affair with my husband."

Andrew shook his head. "Wow. I'm sorry about that. Being betrayed by someone who's supposed to love you hurts like a—well, you know."

I did, but honestly, as I thought about it, I was more angry than hurt. At that moment, anyway.

As I reached the door, I remembered something important and turned back to Andrew. "One more thing. Do you know who Hannah Wyatt is?"

Andrew pressed his lips tight, then said, "No, I don't. Sorry."

"No problem and thanks again."

When we got back in the truck, my phone chimed. A message from *my* contractor. He wanted me to meet him at Break Thyme first thing in the morning.

Good news? I replied.

I wouldn't call it that, but not a surprise. See you at 8?

Sure. Not good news, but I didn't have the energy to worry about it and would deal with it tomorrow. I put my phone away.

"Sounds like Bryan picked a real winner to get mixed up with," I said, bewildered as to how blind he'd been. It seemed like he'd gotten into bed with a devil and taken me with him.

Toni squeezed my hand. "I suppose Andrew could be a suspect in her death after what she did to him, although there's no explanation for why he'd waited so long to get revenge."

"Yes. True. He seemed genuine and too smart to risk everything to kill an ex-wife. My guess is he's moved on."

"Yes, I think so, too. It also doesn't sound like Beverly's sister is the mystery woman, although we can't rule her out. What we know for sure is that whoever approached you in the park, impersonating a dead woman, shouldn't be trusted. If she comes back, that is."

"Yes, of course." What kind of lunatic impersonated the dead? As I had that rational thought, I remembered Beverly had never ventured out from behind the bench. Was that because she was hovering above the ground like a ghost? I would not share that ridiculous thought. The mind went to strange places under stress. Besides, I had a matter of greater concern to consider. "She said she had evidence that would absolve Bryan. Absolve him of what? He was home on Saturday night, so he didn't kill Beverly." Deep down, I believed that, but I still told Toni that I'd found Bryan in his office in the middle of the night.

"So you know for sure he was home," she said.

"Yes. Unless..."

"What?"

"You don't think he could have been awake because he'd gone out, do you?"

"What are you saying, Quinn? Do you think Bryan could have killed Beverly?"

"No." The answer had come flying out of my mouth, confirming I truly didn't think Bryan had killed anyone. But that didn't mean the two of us weren't suspects. "But I can't be sure the police believed me, so I still want to know what Beverly was talking about."

"Quinn, does it matter? You can't trust that woman." Toni handed me a chocolate.

"I know and thanks." I unwrapped a caramel-colored, heart-shaped chocolate with tiny paddles painted on it. A genuine work of art. I showed it to Toni.

She smiled. "You're not the one up a creek without a paddle."

"I hope not. Symbolic though, isn't it?" I said, biting into the sweet heart and chewing it into nothingness. When I finished it, I realized I'd forgotten to enjoy it.

"I will not be blindsided again," I said, emphatically. It was my nature not to leave things to chance. Typically, I was a person who over-prepared for everything and this situation could be disastrous for me as well as my family. I had to arm myself with as much information as possible. "I certainly don't trust that woman, but I want to know if she's holding something over Bryan. He's the father of my children, and I don't want them hurt. I also need to be sure this will not bite me in the butt." How was I supposed to focus on Break Thyme's opening with this mess looming over me?

"Okay, I get that. The two Beverlys are related in some way, so maybe we should try to figure out what thieving Beverly did to get herself murdered."

"I agree," I said. "Shall we find some place for dinner and figure out our next move?"

"Sounds good to me, Sherlock, and you can count on me to be your Watson and for the important stuff like keeping us in chocolate."

Chapter Seven

WHEN I WOKE THE next morning, I was amazed I remembered I had a meeting with Ray, my contractor. I showered, dressed, and drove into town.

A cobblestone alleyway ran between my café and May Flowers, one of Bookend Bay's oldest businesses. Ruby kept the family flower shop pristine and was out front sweeping the sidewalk. Plaited, her red hair hung in a long braid tied with a blue ribbon. Colorful, chunky necklaces swayed as she bent to move a planter.

I waved to get her attention.

"Hello, Quinn. How's the renovation coming?"

"I believe everything is on track for opening day." At least I hoped so. I'd been trying not to worry about Ray's news. He was due to arrive in thirty minutes.

Ruby cradled the broomstick against her chest. "I'll have your potted herbs all ready for your opening."

"Thanks so much, Ruby." In keeping with my herbal theme, I planned to scatter the pots throughout the café.

"My pleasure. We're pleased as punch to have you for our neighbor."

I smiled. She said this every time I saw her. It was no secret she'd not gotten along with the previous tenants, The Peppers. The only thing I knew about the family who'd leased the building before I took over was that they'd run their diner into the ground. There'd been nothing salvageable in the kitchen. Everything was decades old and should have been replaced years ago, so I'd had the kitchen gutted.

"Harriet Pepper wouldn't have stopped to say good morning if her life depended on it. Can you imagine that? It was no wonder they had no customers. Things will sure be different for you."

No customers. My worst nightmare. "I sure hope so."

Ruby reached into her pocket and showed me two nails. "Just so you know, the men who've been working for you dropped these on the sidewalk in front of your place. It was a good thing I noticed them. I wouldn't want anyone to hurt themselves."

"You sure have an eagle eye. Thanks for picking them up." I took a step toward my café. "Have a great day, Ruby."

"You too, Quinn."

I waved hello to Mr. and Mrs. Brooks, who seemed to walk miles every day, then I unlocked the front door to Break Thyme. Instead of buying a new door, I'd had this one sanded down and painted an aquamarine blue.

Inside, the smell of sawdust and some kind of epoxy hung in the air, but it didn't bother me. Every step of this project was a thrill. I was getting closer to opening day. With my next breath, I could almost smell the smooth, dark roast of the finest coffee beans on the market. I'd sourced the best beans I could find and considering the cost of my new coffeemaker, I couldn't wait to taste the first brew.

Since we were keeping the blinds closed during the renovation, I turned on the lights and took it all in. This was mine! I pictured happy customers chatting, drinking, and eating treats.

During the summer season, I planned to serve a new scone each month, themed after an herb. For opening day, I'd offer a citrus glazed, blueberry and lemon-thyme scone. Toni had offered to help with the baking.

I'd hired a professional designer to create an efficient layout and a brand for Break Thyme. In the main café, we'd kept the original wood floors and removed the plaster on one wall to reveal exquisite coral-colored bricks. A staircase led to a loft where I'd have an office and storeroom. A clear, acrylic stair railing kept the space open and the wall exposed.

Opposite this were four booths, reupholstered in a soft gray tweed-looking vinyl. The middle of the room had space for a few tables, leaving an unencumbered path to the counter.

I ran my hand along the smooth, cool finish of the textured steel counter. Made from recycled metal, it was an environmentally friendly choice.

At the back of the café, two steps led down into the Cozy Nook, my favorite part of the café, where construction was still taking place. The new windows provided a breathtaking view of the lake. I'd wanted the barrier between the outdoors and indoors to be as transparent as possible, and I thought I'd achieved that nicely as I took in the cobalt blue water sparkling like precious gems.

The Nook was half the size of the main café which gave it the coziness I wanted. White walls reflected the sunshine.

I loved the crackle of a wood-burning fireplace, but a real fireplace wasn't practical. It would mean having chopped wood on hand and my staff stoking the fire, as well as whipping up specialty drinks. Instead, I'd put in a gas fireplace.

I pictured the room completed with comfy seating, padded footstools and rag-woven baskets filled with throw blankets, from our local Lulu's Creations. The flicker of candles and scented diffusers to keep the air moist. Shelves with books and magazines to read. This would be more than a coffee shop. I wanted this to be a refuge where small, nurturing touches reminded people to be good to themselves.

Pulling myself from my internal reverie, I went to check that my new industrial refrigerator had arrived. In the kitchen, I saw something colorful sitting on the counter.

What was this?

I picked up the painted stone about the size of a mango. At first, I thought it was a scene of Bookend Bay, but as I looked closer, I saw differences. In the painting, a road separated the shops from the water, and the town was nestled between sharp cliffs.

The detail was superb. I didn't know anyone who painted like this and couldn't imagine who'd left it there.

With my mother being scammed, the mystery woman in the park, my marital breakdown, and the appearance of this painted stone, I started to feel numb again. *Just focus on one thing today—Break Thyme.*

I laid the stone down and checked out the refrigerator. Everything looked good. Standing back, I caught a movement through the window in the back door and saw Ray approaching. From the look on his face, I wondered how much worse the day was about to get.

Chapter Eight

Ray gestured to the new windows in the Cozy Nook. "So, what do you think?"

"Absolutely stunning. I love them."

"I'm glad to hear it." He removed his cap and ran his hand over his brown, bald head. "I'll be emailing you the invoice for the beam we put in to support the second story."

"How much."

"The whole shebang will be an extra twenty-five hundred."

I'd told Ray to go ahead with the windows and invoice me later. Still, I grimaced at the extra cost, hearing Bryan's accusation echo in my head that my café was a money pit. "I understand, Ray. It'll be worth it." And I believed that. This room now had a wow factor.

"I agree with you," he said. "The only other shop with an expansive view of the lake like this is the Black Cap and Bib. That diner is busy as all get out."

"I know. It's one of the reasons I wanted these windows."

For a few seconds, Ray's gaze followed a motorboat jetting into open water. "Good investment, in my opinion. I think you're sitting on a gold mine here. You're going to do well, Quinn." He looked at his watch. "We'll get the floor down in this Nook of yours in a couple of days. I've got to get going now. Gotta see Hilda for a teeth cleaning."

"Sure. Just one thing before you go, Ray. Did you or one of your workers leave a painted rock on the counter?"

"What? Painted with what?"

"A beach scene."

He looked at me like I was out of my mind. "No."

"Never mind. I'll figure it out. Thanks for coming by."

After Ray left, I stood alone in my café, baffled by who could have left that painted rock. I figured whoever did it would make themselves known, eventually.

I sat on the stairs, feeling disheartened that Bryan had never been as optimistic about my café as my contractor. If I was being honest with myself, even before Bryan had his nauseating dalliance, I'd questioned whether I wanted to spend my golden years with a man whose priorities were so misaligned from mine. It had been impossible to find common ground. I had to believe, as Ray did, that my café would be a success. This venture had exhilarated me from the start. It had to be right. Why couldn't Bryan see that?

I was going around in circles and needed to touch base with my mother, so I called her. "Hi, Mom. How are things there? I hope you've not had any more bad news."

"Hello, sweetheart. I wish that was the case too, but the toll keeps growing."

"Oh no. I don't understand how the thieves are so convincing."

"Me neither, and I also didn't understand how the scam worked, so I did some research."

I got my curious nature from my mother. The Internet fed her need for constant learning.

She continued. "Do you know these scammers set up fake websites to trick people into giving them their email addresses and private details? That's probably how they got me. These bad guys are crafty. For example, they can make a website look just like it belongs to the government. Now, I know you must check the URL to be sure it's correct because sometimes the address is off by a letter or two. And we should always look for a little padlock beside the address. That's how you know the site is safe."

"Okay, I didn't know that."

"Neither did I. At some point, they fooled me, and the bums got my email address and password. When this happens, you're cooked. They get into your email and change the reply settings, then off they go, sending out fake emails asking for money."

"So when Myrtle got that email, she thought she was replying to you, but she was talking to the scammer."

"That's right. That's when they told her to buy gift cards, scratch and reveal the redemption code, and send the details to them." Mom let out a heavy breath. "Do you know that when two of my friends went to the store to buy gift cards, the clerks warned them they were being scammed? Both my friends ignored the warning and did it anyway."

I could hear the guilt in her voice. "Mom, it's not your fault. Was Jordan not able to get a message out to your contact list?"

"He just called me ten minutes ago. He's still trying."

I knew Jordan was stressed over a project he was finishing up, so I wouldn't push him. "He's been busy, Mom."

"I know it. I could hear it in his voice. I told him to just leave it. Honestly, it's been an education, and I'm not giving them any more of my precious time. Life is too short, honey. None of my friends lost amounts that will change their lives. Hopefully, it's a lesson learned."

"That's a good way to look at it."

"I thought so, too." I heard the smile in her voice. "How's your café coming along?"

I didn't tell her about Bryan. She didn't need that right now. We talked for another twenty minutes and by the time we disconnected, we were both feeling better. She'd been thrown for a loop, but my mother always returned to the sunny side of life. I promised myself to follow her example.

Before heading home, I had one more task to do at the café. Armed with a tape measure, I reached underneath the counter to measure the depth of the shelves to buy the right-sized baskets to store coffee mugs. With the dimensions in my head, I stood to make a note on my phone.

Beverly Foster, the impersonator, was standing on the other side of the counter. My heart hit the roof as a shriek ripped from my throat.

"What are you doing in here? You scared me half to death!" I said. Hadn't I locked the door? And how had I not heard her enter? "I'm not open. Get out."

"I couldn't stay away, Quinn. Not now. Not when something vital has been left undone."

I had my phone in my hand. "I don't want to hear about it. If you don't leave now, I'm calling the police. What kind of nutbar pretends to be a dead woman?"

She shook her head as if I was the deranged one. "You don't get it. I am Beverly Foster. I'm not pretending to be a dead woman. I am dead. You're the only one who can see me."

I had nothing to say to that. Who would? She was wacko. It was time to call the men in white coats.

She glided backward in a smooth, effortless way.

Everything about her was pale—even her clothes—and they were the same ones she'd worn in the park. Same dress. Same lemon scarf. Was she homeless?

"I'm not impersonating anyone," she said. "You are talking to a ghost. I need you to accept that. Look, there's a bullet hole in my back."

As she turned, all the hairs on my body raised in alarm. An unaccountable current skittered across my skin. A cry tore out of my throat as I caught sight of what did indeed look like a bullet hole.

Adrenaline put my flight instinct into hyper-drive. I turned and crashed into a ladder. My forehead stung as I burst into the kitchen. I slammed the door closed and jabbed the hook into the latch. Locked. I bolted across the kitchen to the exit.

Shoot! My keys. I didn't have my purse. I took a breath and turned around.

She was standing in the kitchen, hands on her hips. She'd come through the latched door!

"How did you—? No, this can't be!" My voice came out half-cracked.

"You can try to run away from me, Quinn. I have nothing to do but haunt you day and night...unless you help me."

How could my life have taken such a turn in twenty-four hours? "Why are you doing this to me?"

"Isn't it obvious? First, you can see me. Second, because you're rare."

"I'm the rare one? Have you had a look at yourself lately?"

She chuckled. "Did you know you have two auras?"

"What? No. How would I know that?"

"I've always seen auras, but I've never seen ones like yours." She scrutinized me. "You can tell a lot about a person from their aura."

"Really? You can tell a lot about a person from their behavior, too." Homewrecker.

"Your brightest aura is orange. This tells me you're honest and good-hearted."

I was pretty sure she meant these qualities to be of benefit to her.

"You also have a silver aura," she said, moving closer to me, making me feel like a prime specimen. "If I'm not mistaken, it's growing brighter. People with silver auras are often sensitive and psychic."

"Sensitive enough to see you, unfortunately."

She tilted her head. "You're going through a change, and it's going to make you special, quite special, I believe."

I was going through a change all right, like every other woman my age. I had no wish for an education in auras. "I went to see Andrew Hill this morning," I said and waited for her reaction. If she truly was Beverly's spirit, she should give something away.

Her face turned ghoulishly pale. Ha! That gave me immense satisfaction. Touché. Take that, ghostie.

I hit her with another truth. "He had a few things to say about your character, so you'll understand why I won't be doing you any favors."

"You can't believe everything you hear." She drifted over to the shelving unit I used to store supplies. "And another thing. I may be new at the afterlife, but I'm not without influence. There are some bad spirits around, corruptible spirits, ones just looking for trouble. I could bring them here for a visit."

Could she do that? I didn't want to find out.

"Who is Hannah Wyatt?" I asked.

"I'll tell you when you get the keys. Do it fast, Quinn, before someone else finds them."

"Did you sleep with my husband?" There. I'd drawn the courage to ask the question.

"I see what you're up to. You want something, too. As a show of good faith, I'll tell you what you want to know, then you'll do me that little favor."

My intuition prickled. She wasn't trustworthy, and I needed the truth. Was it enough to know Bryan had come close? Was our marriage salvageable either way?

"I'll get your keys." I said, meaning I'd do it if I was confident Beverly wasn't sending me into trouble. I took a deep breath, steadying my nerves.

She just dropped her shoulders in a sign of relief. "Your husband is corruptible, but it will look otherwise."

Chapter Nine

Your husband is corruptible, but it will look otherwise.
These words rang ominously in my ears. What did that
mean? Look otherwise to who? To me? Our children?
The police? When will it look otherwise? What's going to
happen? Did corruptible mean he'd lied to me, and they'd
had sex? Did corruptible mean he'd been heading in that
direction? Or did it mean something unrelated to sex?

I asked, but Beverly wouldn't elaborate—not until I'd
retrieved her set of keys. Our conversation ended in a
standoff with her fading away.

I had no reason to trust that tart, that tramp, that hussy
spirit. And I had no reason to do her bidding, and I told
her that.

I realized I was shivering and hugged myself tight. A
ghost. I'd been talking to a ghost who'd threatened to
recruit nasty ghosts to haunt me.

I'd never felt this close to neurosis. I needed to calm
down. Somehow, stay sane. *Think normal thoughts.*

My hair was going to need a cut soon, I said to myself,
as I scooted from my creepy kitchen, turned on all the
lights, and retrieved my purse. I should get out of here.

My cat needed me, and *that* was how my life was perfectly normal. I had two beautiful, independent adult kids. Normal.

But then I stood in the Cozy Nook where I'd envisioned happy, relaxed, gratified people. *This was my dream, for crying out loud.* Was I going to let some deadbeat ghosts tarnish this space and make it feel creepy? No. "Screw you, Beverly!" Yelling at her, even in her absence, felt remarkably invigorating, so I cursed her a few more times before locking up and leaving.

I focused on driving safely and was relieved to get home. As I walked in the door, I heard the thump of Oreo's feet hitting the kitchen floor, probably from the window seat where he took in the afternoon sun. He pranced over to greet me, threading himself through my legs as I hung my coat, careful not to trip over him.

"I'm glad you're here, buddy," I said, reaching down to rub under his chin and down his back. His fur was like angora, soothingly soft. Hairs dispersed through the air. He could always use a good brushing.

I followed him into the kitchen and did as his demanding meows directed me. Maine Coons were big eaters. He circled and looked up at me.

"Yes, yes, it's coming." When I'd filled his food bowl, I grabbed my purse and sat at the kitchen table.

"Toni was right. Moments like these require chocolate," I said to my cat, who appeared to have no opinion on the matter. I grabbed my purse to retrieve the foil-wrapped deliciousness Toni had dropped in there.

I'd been debating whether to call Toni to tell her I'd had a conversation with a dead person. So far, the answer was no. First, Toni was at work. Since she'd taken the day off yesterday to spend with me, I didn't want to interrupt her today. Second, it wouldn't be fair to drop something like that in a phone call, so I'd wait until we were face-to-face. And third, I needed to find the right words or perhaps the confidence to admit to something like this. It wasn't that I was worried Toni wouldn't believe me. Or was I? Bryan wouldn't, not in a million years, but Toni knew I wouldn't make up such a bizarre story. I just had to get my own head around this before sharing it with my friend.

Ten minutes later, I was still staring at the foil wrapper, trying, unsuccessfully, to focus on something else besides Beverly's ghost. Of course, everything about her blasted me out of my comfort zone, but I was most disturbed by the unknowns. What did she mean about Bryan being corruptible? What evidence did she have to absolve him? Did that evidence point to the actual killer? Did she know who'd shot her in the back? Did the police consider me a suspect? Who was Hannah Wyatt? The questions kept revolving.

I'd sure gotten a reaction when I'd told her I'd talked to Andrew. Having the upper hand was a good thing, so I was going to do more digging.

Bryan had met her at his late colleague Jim's funeral. I remembered Bryan saying there'd been such a small turnout at the service, he could have skipped it like most of the bank's staff had. Beverly must have been somebody significant to Jim, so maybe I could reach out to Jim's family and learn something about her.

Since I didn't know Jim's last name, I looked up obituaries in our county. They were listed alphabetically, so I started at the beginning.

There were four people under A. I had to click on each one to determine their gender and date of death. This was going to take a while. I grabbed a bottle of wine and used my favorite gadget—a wine aerator—to enhance the flavor of the inexpensive wine.

I was on my second glass when I found Jim Plasky. His profile confirmed he'd worked at the same bank as Bryan and was survived by his wife, Ruth. I found her phone number on the White Pages website.

No time like the present. I entered her number into my phone. A woman answered on the third ring.

"Hi, there. Is this Ruth Plasky?" I asked.

"Yes, it is." Her voice was wheezy, like she'd run for the phone.

"My name is Quinn Delaney. Your husband Jim worked with my husband Bryan."

"Is that right? I remember your husband. He came to Jim's funeral. We sure appreciated him making that effort. He was the only one who attended from the bank."

"Well, Bryan wouldn't have missed it."

"You know, Jim worked there for thirty-five years. They did send a nice flower arrangement though." She hesitated and then sniffed. "What can I do for you?"

I hoped I wasn't upsetting her. "I'm wondering if you can tell me about Beverly Foster. My husband met her at

Jim's funeral." If I was lucky, Beverly was a family member and Ruth would know who Hannah Wyatt was.

Silence.

"Hello? Ruth, are you there?"

"Yes, I am. I just wasn't expecting a question like that."

I realized how insensitive I'd been. "I'm sorry. I should have been more considerate. Of course, you've just suffered her loss, too." No wonder she was sniffling.

"Oh? She died, did she? Well, I'm sorry to hear that."

I guessed Ruth wasn't a big news consumer. My hope for dirt on Beverly diminished considerably. "I guess you didn't know Beverly very well."

"I'll admit, this is a little embarrassing," Ruth said and sneezed. "You'll have to pardon me. My allergies are terrible."

I waited for her to blow her nose. Then she said, "I don't know Beverly at all. My daughter hired her."

That took me by surprise. "She hired her? To do what?"

Ruth sighed. "Beverly was a professional mourner."

I must have heard her wrong. "Did you say professional mourner?"

"Yes, I did."

"I didn't know there was such a thing."

"Well, we have no family. Jim was a bit of a social recluse. He didn't have friends. The funeral home asked if we'd like to hire Beverly to play the part of a grieving cousin to say nice things about Jim. I'm sorry. I know how this sounds..."

Bizarre and shifty—two words that perfectly described Beverly Foster. "There's no need to explain. I understand,

Ruth." I looked back to Jim's profile on the obituary website to see he'd been at Nodsworth Funeral Home.

"Thank you for your time," I said. "I appreciate you talking to me."

"Please don't tell any of your husband's work associates about Beverly."

That would not be a problem. "Don't worry. I won't say a word. I hope your allergies get better. Take care."

"You, too. Goodbye."

I disconnected and contemplated this new information. Beverly Foster was an impersonator, an actor, a deceiver of grieving folks. Had this gotten her killed?

My stomach rumbled for dinner as I scribbled Nodsworth Funeral Home on a notepad, and while I was at it, I made notes on our conversation with Andrew Hill. I wondered if Bryan knew the bombshell he'd fallen for was an impostor. Probably not.

I hadn't heard from him and wasn't missing him one bit. I supposed he hadn't been arrested for Beverly's murder. In this case no news was good news.

This thing with Beverly was getting more outlandish than I ever could have predicted, but I felt confident in my next step; and I wasn't going to stop until I got to the truth, even if I was tempting Beverly's ghostly wrath upon me as a legion of demons. This was my life, and I would not let dead people mess it up.

Chapter Ten

THE NEXT MORNING, I drove to Nodsworth Funeral Home. The Colonial mansion sat on a manicured lawn next to a cemetery on a curvy street of sprawling homes on the west side of the river. Having been to visitations over the years, I was familiar with the funeral home.

Inside, the air smelled of flowers and burning candles. As I walked across the foyer, the carpet felt plush underfoot. A sniffle came from the room to my right as I walked toward the office.

The office was empty. As I exited, a woman in a navy suit walked toward me from the stairway. Having been to the funeral home a few times, I knew the kitchen and restrooms were downstairs.

"Hello," she said with the sympathetic compassion one gives the bereaved. "I'm Joyce, a funeral director, here at Nodsworth. Can I help you?"

"Hello Joyce, I'm Quinn."

Joyce gave a soft nod. "I want you to know we are committed to serving you and your family in every way we can, whether you choose a traditional funeral for your loved one, a simple cremation, or a celebration of life. Would you like to sit down while we talk?"

"You're very kind, and Nodsworth is certainly a lovely home, but I'm not here for your services."

"Oh? What can I help you with then?"

"I'm looking for information about a woman who was referred to a colleague of my husband's. Her name was Beverly Foster."

Joyce opened her mouth, about to say something, but then pressed her lips tight. Too late. I'd already seen the disapproval in her eyes. She made an impatient sound. "Are you here to complain, because we're not responsible for that woman."

"No. That's not why I'm here." Although I was intrigued. I figured Joyce would be more forthcoming if she felt I was an ally. She might even be sympathetic if I told her a little of the truth. "Please. I'm not here to cause any trouble. I'm trying to understand what kind of relationship Beverly had with my husband. Anything you can tell me about her would help."

"Your husband? I see." She didn't look terribly surprised.

"Can I ask you what the complaint about Beverly was about?"

Joyce moved into the office, so I followed.

"You seem like a good person," she said in a lowered voice. "I'll tell you an observation of mine about that woman. She used charm like a weapon to manipulate people and serve herself. Whatever happened with your husband, you can bet he was taken in by her. I know it takes two to tango, but that woman..." Joyce glanced toward the doorway. "She sure had our director under her spell. He was adamant the accusation against Beverly bore no truth."

"What was she accused of doing?"

"Are you aware of the service Beverly provided?"

"I was told by one of your customers she was a professional mourner."

Joyce scoffed. "I never approved. It's, well, to call a duck a bird of prey—it's misleading at the least, an outright lie at its worst."

"Er," I uttered, trying to follow her.

"At any rate, one of our clients hired Beverly to attend a service for his aunt. Apparently, Beverly and a family member, a married man, connected at the funeral."

This sounded familiar.

"This man said his relationship with Beverly became intimate, then in a matter of weeks, he received a—"

"Hello there," a lanky man said who'd come into the office. "I'm one of the directors here at Nodsworth—Gunner Olsen. Can I be of assistance?" My first thought was that he didn't suit his name. To me, Gunner suggested a muscular, bad boy type. Tall and thin, he had wispy hair and wore rimless glasses. He looked like the perfect model of a funeral director.

Joyce turned to acknowledge him. "Yes, you can. This is Quinn." She gestured to me.

"Hi. I'm looking for information about Beverly Foster. She met my husband at a funeral. I understand the family of my husband's colleague hired her as a mourner."

"Since this matter concerns Quinn's husband, I was telling her about Larry Lewis and his complaint against—"

"That's accommodating of you, Joyce," Gunner said with what sounded like sarcasm. "I'll take it from here."

She winked at me. "Fine. Nice to meet you, Quinn, and good luck to you." Joyce walked away quickly.

I silently repeated the name Larry Lewis a few times to get it into my memory.

"I'm sorry about that," Gunner said.

"There's nothing to apologize for. Joyce was telling me about a married man Beverly Foster met at a funeral. It sounded as though an affair came from this meeting. There was a complaint?"

"It proved to be nothing. Beverly, God rest her soul, had done nothing wrong, nothing at all. Please don't think we didn't take the complaint seriously because we did. I talked at length about this with Beverly and listened to everything the man in question had to say."

Gunner cleared his throat. "Unfortunately, for him, it became clear he had a reputation for affairs. When Beverly rebuffed his advances, the gentleman grew agitated and started to harass her. It got quite ugly. Beverly had texts to support her side of things. Eventually, it all died down."

"I got the impression from Joyce that she had reason to believe the man."

"Working relationships are often complex, no? Jealousy and competition over wage differences played a part here. I wish it wasn't the case, but Joyce never liked Beverly. A beautiful woman, often the object of attention, she spurred envy in Joyce and not on purpose. The directors here will miss Beverly even if Joyce does not, and I do sympathize with Joyce. Insecurity isn't an easy cross to bear."

He was in the correct vocation, all right. Gunner had a way about him. Diplomatic and caring, his manner epitomized compassion. I couldn't imagine why he would fabricate a story like this, but I had to admit, a part of me had been more satisfied with Joyce's take on things, especially since I knew there had been a liaison between Beverly and my husband. *Your husband is corruptible.*

"Thank you for explaining. I appreciate you taking the time."

"Of course." He dipped his long fingers into his pocket and retrieved a business card. As he handed me the card, his shirt sleeve pulled up off his wrist, revealing a tattoo that said Loyalty or Death.

I read the words aloud. "That's a rather serious statement." And perhaps grievous for a funeral director.

"Ah, it's not what you think. It's a reference to our Lord who has my loyalty—always."

"I see. Well, thank you, again."

He nodded toward the business card in my hand. "If you have any further questions, please call me directly."

Apparently, he didn't want me talking to Joyce about it. I wondered why that was. "I will, and thanks again. Goodbye." I was heading toward the exit when he called my name. I turned.

"It's not my place to interfere in your marriage. I don't know your husband, but I am psychic, and usually quite accurate, so I want to share something with you, if you would like?

"Sure." Last week, I would have said I didn't believe in psychics, but I couldn't say for sure what I believed in anymore.

"I believe you're a good person, Quinn. I get a strong sense you're standing on a cusp, as if you're about to make a dramatic, life-changing choice. If it's to do with the relationship between your husband and Beverly, I know their association was innocent." He narrowed his gaze, studying me. "But that won't be at the root of it. This change has everything to do with you following the path that brings you joy. Do that, Quinn, and your life will be better than you could ever imagine."

I smiled. "You sound like an inspirational meme, Gunner."

He laughed. "Have a nice day, Quinn."

Sure, after those departing words? I had so much to tell Toni, although I couldn't say I'd resolved anything about Beverly or Bryan. I didn't believe Gunner's assessment of the situation. It seemed to me it behooved him to say Beverly was innocent of wrongdoing.

Joyce made it sound like Larry Lewis received something that prompted his complaint against Beverly. So, my next step was to track him down and find out what really went on between him and the not-so-innocent bombshell.

Chapter Eleven

I T HAD BEEN TWO days since Bryan and I had spoken. We'd never gone this long without speaking. I could have called or sent him a text, but I didn't. I believed he should make the first move, since this was his transgression.

This gap in our communication was both disconcerting and enlightening. First, it didn't look like he was trying to repair our marriage. A part of me was angry about that, but a bigger part was relieved. For two days, I didn't have to carefully consider my words before they left my mouth to avoid an argument. This constant editing was tiring and had been going on even before I decided to open a café. Now that I thought about it, Bryan had never supported my desire to work outside the home. At first, his resistance had been subtle. He'd change the subject or find a home project that needed doing. And I, always one who loved a project, got it done. Bryan wanted my sole focus to be on him and our household. Why had I not seen this clearly before? When I'd moved ahead on the café, he'd gotten physical with another woman.

Anger boiled inside me again. I didn't want these thoughts to ruin my day, so I grabbed my basket of cleaning products, turned on loud music, and scrubbed the bathrooms until my phone rang.

It was my designer calling to say the outdoor chairs we'd chosen for Break Thyme's patio had been discontinued. I needed to review options. I said I'd get back to her.

The music and the energy I spent cleaning had put me in a better state of mind. The day was sunny and cool, so I threw on a wool sweater and took my laptop outside to the deck off my kitchen. Looking over the railing, I noticed the garden below needed watering. Another thing to add to my list.

I still hadn't talked to Toni about ghost Beverly. Toni had sent me a text last night to say her mom needed her to help move furniture for the painters, so we'd try to connect later that evening.

By noon, I had new chairs selected and a raging headache. I'd forgotten to have a coffee that morning. I never forgot coffee.

I opened the French doors, stepped into my kitchen, and was greeted by the aroma of brewed dark roast. I had no memory of making coffee.

Oreo shook himself awake and bounced down off the window seat. He pranced over to me and rubbed his back against my legs, flicking his substantial tail. I looked over at his bowl—it was still full of kibble. I gave his head a scratch. So, I'd remembered to feed the cat and make coffee, but I forgot to drink it?

I really was discombobulated, or did I have a coffee-making poltergeist? Oh, sure. An evil spirit wouldn't brew me a cup when I most needed it.

I heaved a sigh, poured coffee into a mug, added cream, and headed back outside to send my choice of chairs to my designer. Then, I remembered the garden and went downstairs to haul out the hose and water the herbs.

I started with my abundant mint—spearmint, peppermint, licorice mint, orange mint and lavender mint. I'd be clipping herbs frequently to use in my mocktails at Break Thyme. Over the last few years, I'd been experimenting with scone recipes and planned to bake lavender scones with lemon curd later that day.

I was watering the dill and lemon balm when I heard my son's bellow. "Mom. Where are you?" I laughed to myself. Always a kid.

I would not yell back to him. With his long legs, he'd be through the house in seconds.

"There you are," Jordan called from the deck. He skidded down the stairs. Sometimes I wondered how much time his feet spent connected with the ground.

I turned off the hose.

"Hello, my love." I wrapped my arms around his shoulders, relishing the feel of him, his unique scent, the scruff of his beard against my face. My son was nearly a foot taller than me. With his long hair tied back, hair the color of beach sand I used to tell him, he looked like a hippie throwback.

"Hello, my mother," he said, releasing me to pull an apple from his pocket. "Want a bite?"

"Sure." I bit in, perfectly ripe and full of juice. With juice dribbling down my chin, I handed the apple back.

He indicated my dribble with a nod. "That's not a good look for you."

I wiped my chin with my sleeve. "I've cleaned a good amount of juice from your chin, laddie boy." I was a little concerned by his showing up in the middle of the day and hoped he hadn't been talking to his father and learned Bryan was staying elsewhere.

"Ancient history. I gotta get back to work in a few but wanted to tell you I got Gramma's contact list back. I set her up with a new email address."

"Oh, that's good news. Thank you. She appreciates you taking the time to help her when you're so busy."

"Of course I'd help Grammy. She probably wiped up my dribble, too." He took another bite of his apple and chewed while I watered a pot of basil.

"So, I've got other news," he said.

"Oh?"

"Yeah, I'm taking a vacation."

I wasn't expecting that. "It's about time. I'm really glad to hear it. So, things are calming down at work?"

"A little. I'm just taking four days. Going to Las Vegas with Chelsea."

"Chelsea? Isn't that a little...soon?"

"I don't know, is it? She's fun, and she's available."

Because she doesn't work. But I didn't say that. Instead, I wondered how she was paying for the trip, but Jordan was twenty-seven years old and wouldn't appreciate my asking about Chelsea's bank balance.

"You deserve a break," I said. "When are you leaving?"

"Two days."

"Do you need a ride to the airport?"

"Nah, Chelsea's mom is going to take us."

Oh, Chelsea's mom. "Great."

"Could use a ride home though."

I knew I was being silly, but it felt good to know he needed me. "Text me the details and I'll be there."

Jordan kissed my cheek. "Will do. Gotta jet. Love ya."

At least he looked happy. "Love you, too," I said, and he bounded around the side of the house.

My heart broke at the thought of telling him his parents were splitting up. Were we splitting up?

I couldn't imagine having that conversation with Jordan and Samantha. Sadness engulfed me at the thought. I pushed it away, ignoring reality for the moment and telling myself it would be better for us all if Bryan and I kept our family intact.

Chapter Twelve

JORDAN COULDN'T HAVE BEEN more than half a mile down the road when Beverly the ghost showed up.

"Good grief!" I said, clutching my chest, but recovering quickly. "If it isn't the pestiferous phantom. Come to spread more good cheer, have you?" My voice sounded surprisingly strong and hopefully conveyed I wasn't afraid of her.

Beverly scanned my riverside yard from the herbs I'd just watered to the wrap-around patio shaded by the upstairs deck. "Pleasant home you have." For a second, she looked like she might be tabulating what my house was worth. I could almost see dollar signs in her eyes, probably an old habit because wealth wouldn't benefit her now.

"Quinn, I think we got off on the wrong foot. That's understandable considering the circumstances."

"Circumstances meaning you slept with my husband or that you're dead? I think both are grounds for tenuous footing."

She nodded. "Indeed. My point is I'd like to start over."

"Let's start with this, then. Who killed you?" I asked. She wasn't the only one who could act abruptly. "We both know it wasn't Bryan. I don't believe you have evidence against him."

"Is that a risk you're willing to take? Would it be difficult for your children if their father was accused of murder? Sometimes, an accusation is enough to ruin a family. Who knows, the police might even think you did it."

Anger burbled up inside me, but before I could speak she said, "Don't get me wrong—I don't want any of those scenarios to happen, Quinn." She clutched herself, eyes filling with pain. "The truth is I don't know who shot me in the back." The strangled words curtailed my irritation with her slightly. I didn't like her, but that didn't mean I wasn't empathetic. From what I knew of her, her murder probably wasn't random or for robbery's sake. It was probably personal.

"You have no idea? No enemies? No one you might have angered?" Like the wife of someone else you slept with, I thought, but spared her the accusation. For now.

She looked away, but I'd seen the defiance in her eyes. "There are a few people who wouldn't be running for president of my fan club, but you just need to be concerned with one."

"I trust the police to find your killer," I said, although I'd recently read a statistic that said somewhere between two and ten percent of incarcerations are innocent people.

"Maybe, or they'll blame the wrong person. It happens more than you think. You're confident Bryan's alibi will hold up? I hope you don't lay awake wondering what evidence against your unfaithful husband is yet to be found."

Empathy obliterated. I really didn't like this swindling spirit.

"I'll tell you where to find the truth," she said.

My mood perked. "Okay, but why don't you just tell me the truth."

She ran her fingers along the edge of the butter-yellow scarf fixed loosely around her neck. "Because I need something, too, Quinn. We don't know each other. We don't even like each other, so we're going to have to build trust. You can find proof I'm telling the truth at the library."

She was right, but the library took me by surprise. "Bryan never went to the library."

"I was never much of a reader either, which made the library perfect."

"Perfect for what?"

"I used books to send messages. Look for a book called *The Gifted* by E. Rowe. On page 122, you'll find what you need."

I flashed her a look to let her know how crazy this sounded. "Messages to who? Couldn't you use a phone or email like a normal person, or were you some kind of spy?"

"Phones and emails leave records."

"Who were you communicating with?"

"That's not your concern," she said. "If you're not interested in what your husband has been up to..."

She had me, and she knew it. "What if the book isn't there?"

"I wouldn't send you if it wasn't there."

I'm not sure how long I stood with my mouth hanging open, but it was too long. Beverly faded back into the ether or wherever she'd sprung from. "Wait. Come back here! Is this dangerous?"

I dropped the garden hose. I should have turned it on her as if it would do any good. She was probably laughing at me. Find a message in a book? Even spies surely had more sophisticated communication methods.

Still, whoever Beverly had been, I knew I was going to look for the message. I couldn't resist. When the curiosity genes were being divvied up—I got them all. My family would attest to that.

I put the hose away and went inside to wash. Then, I logged on to the library website and looked up *The Gifted* by E. Rowe. It was a fiction novel shelved in Fantasy Romance, and it was available.

Ten minutes later, I was in my truck heading down Riverside Road. The library was at the corner of Honesty and Courtesy, a big old mansion and one of my favorite places in the whole world.

I parked on a side street and hurried into the library through the heavy, arched door. The wood floor creaked as I walked through the security turnstile. The faint smell of books lingered in the hushed room.

At this time of day, many chairs were filled with seniors reading papers or magazines. The book I was looking for was on the third level, so I headed up the stairs.

By the time I reached the top, my heart had doubled its beats per minute. Not good. I was no couch potato, but this was a reminder I needed to get more cardio. Lately, I'd begun to consider things like healthy aging. As far as aging gracefully went, I wasn't ready to embrace gray hair, not yet. Maybe in another decade or so.

At the top of the stairs, I turned right. Mysteries were my favorite. And who didn't enjoy a good love story once in a while. I walked past the reading rooms, then between two rows of fiction, trying not to get side-tracked by book covers calling out to me.

Within the books penned by authors whose surnames began with R, *The Gifted* was shelved as promised. A tingle of adrenaline hit my bloodstream as if I was doing something risky.

Removing the book, I flipped the pages to find page 122. I was expecting a piece of paper set in the fold, but there was nothing. I held the book upside down and gave it a shake. No secret message fell to the floor. What was I supposed to do with this?

I looked around to see if my menacing spirit was watching her joke play out. No sign of Beverly.

With the book tucked under my arm, I brought it with me to the end of the aisle and sat in a chair by the window where the light was brighter. Once again, I turned to page 122. Looking closer, I now saw something unusual. Circles were penciled around some letters. What in the world had Beverly been up to before she was killed?

Someone nearby cleared their throat. It gave me a start. I looked over to see a man shift his position, his gaze glued to the book in his hand.

I wasn't sure why this was making me so nervous. I wanted to get out of there, so I headed downstairs to check the book out. We still did things the old-fashioned way in Bookend Bay, so I waited in line for a librarian.

"How's it going, Quinn?" she asked, taking my card and the book.

"I'm good thanks, Eliza. And you?" Eliza's mother owned Lulu's Creations, a home décor shop across the street from Break Thyme.

"Fantastic," she beamed. "I've just gotten engaged. See?" She wiggled her fingers in front of me to show off her diamond.

"It's lovely. Congratulations." I didn't elaborate, eager to be out of there.

"After ten years, it better be." She laughed and scanned my card, then picked up the book. She turned it over and then over again. "That's strange. There's no barcode on this book."

That didn't sound good.

"I wonder how it got shelved like that," she said.

I had a pretty good idea how that had happened, but then I remembered I'd looked up the book to find its genre.

"It was in the system," I said. "Can you give it a barcode?"

She read the spine. "*The Gifted* by E. Rowe." Her fingers flew over her keyboard, then she frowned. "I don't see it in the system."

"That's strange." I retrieved my phone to find the page I'd searched. It wasn't there. "I'm sorry. I can't find it, but I'm sure I saw it earlier. I looked up the book's category."

The librarian looked puzzled. *Please, don't let there be a problem.* I needed that book.

"It must be a glitch," she said. "No worries. I'll get it set up."

I exhaled a breath of relief. Three minutes later, I had the book in hand. Outside, I decided to sit at a picnic table and translate the message.

"Hello," I said to Charlie on his way into the library. Charlie and his partner Tucker owned the bookstore.

"Good afternoon, Quinn," Charlie said as I passed. "It sure is a sunny one today." It was customary to greet everyone you walked by. We couldn't very well name our streets after virtues and not be neighborly.

I slowed but kept walking. "It sure is, Charlie. Enjoy your day."

Whatever nerves I'd felt inside dissipated in the outdoors. I found an unoccupied picnic table and shifted my legs over the bench to sit down. I could record the circled letters on the notepad app on my phone. I opened the book to page 122. Starting at the top, left-hand page, I used my finger to scroll across the first sentence, then the next.

In the second paragraph, I found the letter B circled. As in Bryan? I typed B into the notepad. When the next letter was R, I was convinced the message was about my husband.

The third letter was I. That's odd. His name was spelled with a Y, but the name Bryan was also commonly spelled with an I. People made this mistake all the time.

I was now three-quarters of the way down the page where I found the fourth circled letter—M. That made no sense. It should be an A. I went back to find the I and started again from there to see if I'd missed a letter.

I hadn't. I now had Brim. I kept looking for circled letters until I had the word Brimley. Brimley what? I hoped it wasn't referring to Brimley State Park. It was an enormous park, and I couldn't imagine what it had to do with Bryan.

I scoured the text for another letter and found an L. A few minutes later, I had the word life. Brimley Life. I didn't know what this meant, so I kept going. By the time I reached the bottom of page 123, I had Brimley Life Storage Eight.

I looked up Brimley Life Storage and found it actually existed and was twenty-six miles from Bookend Bay in what looked like an industrial area. I supposed eight might refer to a unit, but really, what good was this? How would I get into a storage unit?

If Beverly had evidence that implicated or absolved Bryan in a crime, why didn't she tell me what it was and where to find it? Why put me through this cryptic nonsense?

A spindly flower fell from a tree, landing on the open book. I brushed it away and noticed a faint circle around page number 123.

I sat there, tapping my foot. Maybe 123 was the code for a number pad. It seemed too easy a code for someone to guess. Maybe there were more digits. I slowly flipped the pages, watching the numbers file by.

There! Page 162 was also circled. If there was a number pad to get into a storage unit, the code could be 123162. Maybe.

Or this decoding game was a bunch of baloney. There was only one way to find out.

Chapter Thirteen

IF I WAS GOING to drive to Brimley Life Storage, I better do it now before I lost my nerve. I thought about waiting until Toni was finished work and ask her to come with me, but at the same time, I didn't know what evidence Beverly had. I wanted to see it first.

I also considered calling Bryan, but the thought of seeing him just made me angry. Maybe it was an omen, but I had a feeling I should get used to doing things on my own.

I picked up the book and trekked back to my truck. When my stomach growled, I realized I'd forgotten to eat lunch, so I left the truck and crossed the road to Henrietta's Bakery. I loved that the bakery smelled of sweet deliciousness, but I didn't love the Christmas decorations that were still in place. In May. I ordered a Croque Monsieur sandwich to go. And a chocolate hazelnut tart because the mission I was about to undertake required chocolate.

Every bite was sensational. With my attention on my taste buds, the tension building in my shoulders eased.

Forty minutes later, I drove into the storage complex. Rows of blue garage doors filled the facility, each door had drive-up access. It was a relief to see no sign of life, although there were security cameras in place. I turned down the first row to my left and found a unit designated as number eight.

How would I explain myself if someone asked what I doing there? I'd assumed the unit belonged to Beverly, but I didn't know that for a fact. I supposed I could pretend to be Beverly's relative—a trusted someone since I had the access code.

I glanced at a camera. The longer I lingered, the more likely I'd look like I didn't belong.

I put the truck in park and cut the engine. At the keypad, I punched in 123162. If it didn't work—

I heard the click of a release, and the door rolled up. With a quick look over my shoulder, verifying I was still alone, I entered the unit. Slightly cooler inside, the air smelled musty.

It was a lot of space for the little it contained. Against the back wall was an industrial shelving unit, common in garages. The shelves were empty. In the middle of the floor sat a steel desk with a banker-sized box on top and a folder. I walked over to the desk and reached for the folder.

Wait! My intuitive voice stopped me. Could this be some kind of setup? I'd come at the bequest of a phantom—a murdered woman I'd be stupid to trust. She had her own agenda, and I doubted very much she had a benevolent bone in her body.

There'd been a murder, and there must be an ongoing investigation. Could the police be watching this unit? If they were, it was too late. I'd already have been spotted, so I might as well poke around. If the police weren't watching, then I shouldn't leave fingerprints.

Feeling like I was in a crime detective movie, I scooted back to the keypad and used my sleeve to clean off my prints. At least I hoped a swipe with my sleeve did the trick. I rubbed the keys again—vigorously.

Inside my truck, I kept a set of gardening gloves. Retrieving these, I hurried back to the folder on the desk. Opening it wasn't easy with gloves, but I got it done.

"Good grief!" I said aloud, then looked behind me as if anyone had heard. The folder showed a photo of Bryan. He was standing against the trunk of his car, his gaze on the phone in his hand, a smile on his face. The shot was zoomed in close. The blurred background didn't reveal where the photo was taken.

Another photo was tucked underneath. I took off my gloves. Now that I'd seen these, I planned to take them with me. Bryan was center stage in the next photo, entering The Blackwood Motor Inn. I didn't recognize the motel.

A sick feeling tumbled through my stomach. What had Bryan been doing there? Meeting Beverly? If that was the case, how did these photos prove Bryan was innocent of anything?

I slipped on the gloves and lifted the lid of the box sitting beside the folder. Seeing what was inside, my stomach flipped again.

Money. Stacks of hundred-dollar bills. What the heck was this? I dropped the lid back in place. Whoever put this here it couldn't have been meant for me. Could it?

No. Beverly couldn't have set this up from the grave, so either someone else did this or she did it before she was killed. I knew one thing for sure. I wanted nothing to do with this money. It was creepy and didn't belong to me. On the other hand, I was going to talk to Bryan about these photos.

I was suddenly cold. I grabbed the folder and hurried back into the sun, pulling the door closed behind me. Inside my truck, I did a U-turn to get out of there.

My hands were shaking. I took a deep breath at the end of the driveway and turned onto the road leading back to the highway.

By the time I reached Bookend Bay, I had some choice words picked out for that swindling hobnocker, to borrow one word from my mother. Saying it made me smile.

"Show me what you found," Beverly said, startling me once again, having appeared in the hallway at home after I walked in the door.

"Stop doing that!" People told me I was a patient person. I wasn't quick to anger, but man, Beverly brought my blood to a boil.

I fluttered the folder in front of her face. "You lied to me. These photos don't prove Bryan innocent or guilty of anything."

"Bryan at a motel?"

"Yes, he's at a motel. He could have stopped there for any reason. Maybe he had to use a bathroom?"

"If that's want you want to believe. Did you find anything else of interest?"

"You mean stacks of cash?" I asked. "I will not take cash that doesn't belong to me. Who knows what kind of trouble that would bring."

Beverly smiled. "I was right about you," she said it like a compliment.

"Same here." I didn't mean it as a compliment.

She gave a clipped laugh. "You didn't take the money. I had to know if you were trustworthy, Quinn, because I have something very important that I need you to do. Now I know you're not only resourceful, but you can also be trusted."

The noise that ripped from my throat sounded like a growl. "How dare you send me on a wild goose chase. You want me to do something for you? Well, you can just forget it. You may trust me, but I sure don't trust you."

She didn't look concerned, which worried me. "You could ask Bryan what he was doing at the Motor Inn, and he could tell you a number of innocent lies."

He'd already admitted he'd gotten physical with her, and I didn't need to see evidence of that. Before I could say so, she continued.

"I know exactly what he was doing, and now that we know what was in that storage unit, I'm a bit concerned. That money and those photos could mean Bryan is being set up to take the fall for my murder. Or, and I hate to even think this, you could be the target."

"You hate to think it, do you?" I knew what she was doing. She needed leverage to coerce me into finishing whatever sketchy business she'd left undone. "Get out, Beverly. Get out of my life and don't come back. I won't be manipulated by you. I don't want to see your foul phantom face again."

She made a dismissive gesture. "You need time to think things over. I understand. It's a lot to digest." She glided back toward the door. "Don't wait too long, though. I wouldn't want anything bad to happen in the meantime. I'll be back when you change your mind." With that not-so-subtle threat, she disappeared.

Chapter Fourteen

I'D JUST FINISHED DINNER, baked salmon and roasted vegetables, when I got a call from Ray. He was laying the floor in the Cozy Nook at Break Thyme that week.

"You better get over here right away," he said.

From the tone of his voice, my heart sank. "What's wrong?"

"Just meet me at the café, Quinn, lakeside. You'll have to see this."

Whatever this was, it didn't sound good. *Please don't let this be Beverly's doing.* "Okay, I'll see you soon."

When my life was not in a good place, I made a point to appreciate the little things, anything that was going well. So, on the way to Break Thyme, I told myself how wonderful it was to live in a small town with a six-minute commute to work. Some people suffered hour-long commutes in bumper-to-bumper traffic or on crowded public transportation. Yes, I sure was lucky, and I had a well-running truck to deliver me to whatever disaster awaited.

You don't know it's a disaster. Think positive!

My thoughts boomeranged back to Beverly's threat. I hated it when my mind had a mind of its own. Surely, she had no power to affect anything tangible in my life, and I refused to be coerced by a ghost—especially her.

The more I thought about it, the angrier I got.

Shoot, I was supposed to be in a zen state of gratitude.

The nerve of her—seducing my husband, then demanding I do her bidding. Who the heck did she think she was?

Breathe. Just breathe.

I parked my truck in Moose Harbor's parking lot. From there, I could see most of the shops that ran along Courtesy Boulevard. Break Thyme was the third shop down from the harbor.

I saw a major problem immediately and started to hyper-ventilate.

"No. No. No." I ran toward my beautiful dream, my lakefront café with wall-to-wall picture windows that brought the outside world in.

No. Not like this. Not literally.

A huge tree limb had crashed through my gorgeous windows.

I spit out a few words stronger than hobnocker.

The branch had come from a twin oak tree—one I'd admired. A chunk of that tree was now embedded in my café. Glass was everywhere. I blinked away a tear. One small blessing. My store sign had survived.

Oliver from Ollie's Outfits was standing on the grass beside Ray. They both stopped talking as I approached.

"No one was hurt?" I asked, sounding almost like I had it together.

Ray's brown eyes were full of commiseration. "No. We'd finished for the day."

Oliver shook his head. "Ah, Quinn, I sure am sorry for you. What a mess. I can't say I'm surprised, though. This oak's been losing bark and growing mushrooms for a couple of years now."

"It has?" I said, whatever bark and mushrooms meant. "I didn't notice."

Oliver leaned over and peered, over his long, thin bony nose, at the standing tree. "Parks and rec better send over an arborist to evaluate this." He jabbed at the bark. "That's a bark beetle right there. You don't want those."

"Okay." I said, still stunned. "I think I have a bigger problem right now than bark beetles."

"I hope you have insurance for this kind of thing," he said.

I swallowed and put on a brave face. It was a brick, mortar, and glass. Nothing that couldn't be replaced—at a cost. "I don't own the building, Oliver. I lease it. Surely, I'm not responsible for this."

"Well, you know... They might consider it an act of God," he said.

"You're not helping, Oliver." Out of the corner of my eye, I thought I caught a flash of corn-silk-yellow within the branches of the tree that was still standing. Was that Beverly's scarf? "Act of God, my foot." I marched closer, looked up, but didn't see any sign of her. Maybe it was a trick of the light. Surely, she couldn't fell a tree.

I approached the fallen half. Ray came up behind me. "Don't get too close, now. It's dangerous. Those windows are in a million pieces."

"I see that." I let out a heavy sigh and stepped back. How was I supposed to be ready for opening day now?

"Have you dealt with this kind of thing before, Ray?"

"Not exactly, no," he said. "I'll get my crew to clean up the glass and any damage inside, but you'll have to call a tree removal company—pronto. This is a hazard."

"I'll call the property owner. He'll have to deal with the tree. I don't know if it's his problem or the city's, but I can't believe it's mine."

"You know what? Let me give them a call. I've been doing work on these properties for years. I know Hank pretty well. He'll be home having dinner."

"I'd appreciate that, Ray. Thank you."

"Quinn, don't tell me this is supposed to be your new café?" I turned to see Mary Carscadden standing at a safe distance. Mary owned the Bookend Bay Inn down the street.

I closed the gap between us. "Yes, but I always envisioned it without broken windows."

"I imagine you did. Lord love a duck, you are having a bad week."

I stared at her for a few seconds, wondering how she knew that.

"I'm sorry. I'm talking out of turn," she said.

Then, it occurred to me why she might have an inkling about my dreadful week. "Is Bryan staying at the inn?"

"Yes, he is, and it's none of my business why. I should have kept my mouth shut."

I didn't know Mary well, but our kids had been in school together, and we'd once sat beside each other at a Christmas concert and had a fun time together.

"It's okay, Mary. These things happen. We're just taking a brief break."

"I understand. Sometimes that's the best thing for a marriage. I know that from experience. Once, I ran off to Myrtle Beach to stay with my sister for an entire month. That sure did wonders. My husband had no idea how much work I do every day—they call it invisible work—and he was sure happy to have me back."

I smiled tightly. I didn't want to know what had sent her to Myrtle Beach. I doubted her husband had an affair with a woman who was murdered and then haunted her. Maybe even destroyed a tree because Mary wouldn't do the ghost's bidding. Nope, that probably wasn't it.

"We'll see," I said, trying for optimism. "I have a few other pressing demands on my time."

"That's the truth, all right," said Oliver as he walked past us toward his store. "Good luck, Quinn."

Mary rolled her eyes at Oliver. "Bryan should be here helping you with this, Quinn. Surely he would. Have you called him?"

"No. I just got here myself." I guessed it was telling that I'd not considered calling Bryan—again. I had no faith he wouldn't say I told you so. In his mind, this would be proof my café was destined to fail. "I'm going to handle this myself, Mary. Please don't tell him."

"Okay, then. I won't say a word."

Ray was still on his cell phone. I hoped there wasn't too much damage inside the building. Luckily, there was no furniture that could have been crushed. The room was still under construction.

"Thank you. Excuse me, Mary. That's my contractor over there." I pointed to Ray, who appeared to have finished his phone call. "I'm going to ask him to come inside with me to have a look."

"I do hope this doesn't cause you too much grief," Mary said.

"Me too."

"Just before you go, I think you deserve to know something."

I held my breath. What now? Had she seen Bryan doing something he shouldn't be doing?

"We had a problem with the faucet in Bryan's room, and I had to let in the plumber. I think Bryan is going to be home soon. It looks like he's planning to surprise you with a trip."

I was not expecting that. "Seriously? Did he say that?"

"Well, no, he wasn't there. I saw quite a few travel brochures on the desk. You might find yourself going east."

"East? My mother lives in the Canadian Maritimes."

"No, no, farther east than that. I think he's considering South Korea. Now, wouldn't that be an adventure?"

South Korea? Never in all the years I'd known Bryan had he mentioned traveling to the Far East. I'd hardly been able to get him to leave the country.

"I'm telling you this because you need some cheering up, but don't tell him I let the cat out of the bag."

"Don't worry about that. I won't say a word. Have a great day, Mary."

As I bee-lined it for Ray, I tried to assimilate this new information with what I knew of my husband. Was it possible he was going to surprise me with a trip?

I didn't know what to think other than a trip seemed rather presumptuous, since he hadn't even picked up the phone to ask if I wanted him to come home.

Chapter Fifteen

THE BUTTER KNIFE IN Toni's hand hovered over the bowl of lemon curd I made for our scones. "Let me be clear I've understood. You believe you've been talking to your husband's dead mistress's ghost?" She put the knife down on the table.

We were sitting outside on the patio in my backyard. I'd told Toni I had something serious to discuss and asked her to keep an open mind and not interrupt until I got it all out. Then I told her everything that had happened since Beverly began haunting me. By the time I finished, I was shaking; surprised by how stressful it was to admit to something I wouldn't have believed a month ago.

Toni put her hand over mine. Suddenly I wasn't sure the gesture wasn't to placate a crazy person.

"You're not questioning my mental state, are you?" I said, feeling panicky. If I didn't have Toni's support, I didn't know how I would cope. "You don't think I'm...delusional?"

She squeezed my hand. "Of course not, Quinn. It's not like we just met yesterday. I could tell how difficult it was for you to tell me all this. I'm holding onto you because

I'm freaking out a little, but I'm here for you. We're going to be okay."

Relief washed over me. I reached for her and hugged her tight, feeling guilty that in sharing my burden, I'd unnerved her. "Thank you, and I'm sorry to stress you out."

She leaned back in her chair. "Don't you dare be sorry. We're friends through thick and thin, so if werewolves come howling at my door, you better believe I'm calling you."

I laughed. "Deal."

"Amazingly, I still have an appetite." She picked up her knife and slathered one side of the lavender scone with lemon curd. "So, you haven't spoken to Bryan at all? He knows nothing about Beverly's ghost?"

I'd been so much more confident Toni would believe me than Bryan ever would. The thought of telling him about Beverly's ghost had me tongue-tied. "No, nothing, and I don't plan to tell him. He'd never believe it."

I told her what Mary, the inn owner, said about the travel brochures in Bryan's room. "Mary thinks Bryan is going to surprise me with a trip."

Toni cocked her head. "On one hand, I'd be shocked if that was true, but on the other hand, it's exactly what he *should* do, don't you think?"

It was no secret Bryan didn't like to travel. "It would be an olive branch on his part, a step in the right direction in repairing the damage he's done."

Toni sighed. "Do you miss him?" She took a bite of the scone.

I shook my head, feeling another ripple of guilt, but it was the truth. "When he admitted to his inappropriate behavior with Beverly, I was devastated. I couldn't imagine recovering from that betrayal."

"Can you imagine it now? This scone is perfection, by the way."

"Thank you. That's the thing. Toni, I've got the strangest discordance running through me. On one hand, I've always believed we'd grow old together. On the other hand, there's no together anymore. I know it sounds cliche, but we've been doing our own thing for so many years now, we've drifted apart. It's glaringly obvious now we have nothing in common."

"I understand. I know you've given up trying to find things to do together."

It was true. We didn't like the same things. His idea of fun was to hole up in his man cave with his friend Edward and watch a wresting match while throwing darts. I had nothing against these things, they just didn't interest me.

I liked the outdoors. My idea of fun was the annual camping trip Toni and I took each summer, originally with our kids. While Toni's husband would have been happy to join us, Bryan hated camping, so these adventures became girlfriend time.

"The thing is, I'm okay with Bryan's absence, and whether or not he's planning a trip, it looks like he's not missing me either." I'd even wondered if he was grieving the loss of his lover.

"Mm, hmm," Toni agreed, around another bite of scone. "Back to your swindling spirit. Are you concerned she toppled that tree branch since you said you wouldn't help her? Can ghosts do things like that?"

"My knowledge of ghosts comes from mystery novels, but I don't think so. I just thought I saw her scarf because she'd just threatened me. It was just as likely I saw a goldfinch because if it had been her, she'd have stuck around, so I knew it."

Toni wiped her mouth with a napkin. "That makes sense. And my ghost knowledge is as sparse as yours. Quinn, you've got a lot on your plate right now. Would you mind if I told Colleen about Beverly? If anyone knows about ghosts, it's her. She might have some advice."

Colleen Walsh owned The Mystic Garden, one of the shops on Courtesy Boulevard. She sold crystals, candles, jewelry, essential oils, books, and things related to the supernatural. I'd heard she gave readings, tarot or tea leaves. Something like that. She was always friendly. I imagine she'd be rather accepting of my occultish experience, and it would be great to talk to someone in the know.

"That's a great idea," I said. "Yes, please, if you wouldn't mind." I was glad for the change of subject from my marriage.

"So, when are we meeting this Larry fellow?" Toni asked, already on board. I'd told her that after Louise from the funeral home mentioned Larry's complaint against Beverly, I'd found his number and called him. He seemed enthusiastic about sharing his experience with Beverly, which I found both strange and fortunate. He'd asked to meet at the Black Cap, the diner in town.

Having my friend by my side made me feel like a new person. I checked the time on my phone. "We should leave in ten minutes."

Larry Lewis looked to be in his forties, round-faced, rosy-cheeked, smooth-shaven, and no taller than me at five foot five. He sucked his Pepsi from a straw.

We were sitting in a booth near the back of The Black Cap and Bib, a landmark in Bookend Bay. The decor was black and white in keeping with the chickadee theme of the diner. Little birds were stamped every-where—mugs, curtains, tablecloths, paintings, server's aprons. The birds were cute but overdone in my opinion. I'd been careful not to let Break Thyme's herb theme take over at Break Thyme.

"Listen," Larry said. "When you told me your husband got mixed up with Beverly Foster, I wanted to talk to you, so maybe some good comes out of my experience; for you, that is. If it's not too late."

I glanced at Toni, then back to Larry. "What do you mean, not too late?"

"I'll tell you what happened to me." Larry wiped his brow. This was obviously uncomfortable for him, and I appreciated him sharing what I assumed was a shameful experience.

"I met Beverly Foster at my aunt's funeral last fall. We don't have much family…"

"I know she worked as a hired mourner." I scanned the diner in case a certain spirit was alerted to our discussion about her. I was happy not to see the ghostly bombshell.

"Yeah, that's right," Larry said. "Anyway, we ran into each other about a week after the funeral. At the time, I thought it was one of those random things, but after, I realized it was all part of the setup. At the funeral, I'd told her about my boat. How it always pained me to take it out of the water at the end of the season."

"She ran into you at the marina?" Toni asked.

"Yep. She said she was looking at a Monterey Cruiser for sale. Oh, she had me going, all right. Asked for my opinion on the boat. I spent a couple of hours with her on the cruiser, looking everything over." He smacked his forehead. "She reeled me in, all right."

I wrapped my hands around my mug. Hook, line, and sinker, as they say. "She was a professional. You couldn't have known."

He scoffed and held out his arms. "Look at me. Do you think a gorgeous babe like Beverly goes for a man like me in the real world?"

He had me there. I didn't. "Looks aren't everything."

"Ha! Anyway, I fell for her hard, real hard." He shook his head. "Don't worry, I'll spare you the details. It went on for a couple of months. Oh man, I was walking on a cloud. And then, she didn't answer my texts."

Toni tapped my foot with hers and flicked her eyes toward the door.

Bryan had just walked in. He slid into a booth at the front of the diner. He hadn't seen us, but he was facing our way. Since he wasn't eating at home, it made sense he'd eat at the Black Cap. My mind wandered for a second, wondering what he was thinking and why he hadn't contacted me.

Larry continued, and I focused my attention on him. "Then a package arrived at my house with instructions. My house! My wife Anna could have opened it."

"Instructions to do what?" Toni asked.

"They sent me on a goose chase that led to a storage locker." He swallowed.

I think I swallowed harder.

"They had pictures," he said, confirming my thoughts.

"Oh, dear. I can imagine." I didn't want to know how explicit his photos had been.

Larry reached for his glass. When his hand trembled, he put it back in his lap. "I don't know that you can. At least I hope not."

The server came by and asked if we wanted refills. We didn't.

"These pictures were perverse," said Larry, so quietly I had to lean forward to hear him over the chatter and clinking cutlery. "She doctored them, so it looked like... like I was role playing a sick fantasy."

I grimaced and remembered the article I'd read that said Beverly's body had been found in the garden of a swinger's club. It sounded like the kind of place where fantasies might be played out.

Larry had been avoiding eye contact, but now he looked at me pleadingly. "It wasn't like that. I want you to know it in case you get the same thing delivered to your house."

My chest tightened around my heart. It was bad enough having thoughts of Bryan with another woman. I didn't want photos and falsified ones? Images like that would be impossible to scour from memory. "Did she threaten to show them to your wife?"

"Yeah, at first. I never knew if it was her who sent the photos or if she was working with someone else. She obviously didn't take them, but she could have set up a hidden camera, right? I never heard from her again. The messages came from random numbers."

For everyone's sake, I hoped it was all Beverly's doing, so it would stop with her death. "Did you tell your wife?"

His chin trembled. "I figured I had to tell her, or the blackmailing would never stop. As you can imagine, it ruined my marriage."

"I'm sorry," Toni said, without a great degree of empathy in her tone.

Hunched over, Larry looked small and tired. "We've been trying to patch things up over the last month or so. She's so much better than I deserve."

"People make mistakes," said Toni, softening.

"I just hope mine is forgivable, one day."

I glanced over at Bryan's booth. His head was down, probably reading the news on his phone. I wasn't in a forgiving mood, not yet. Not after hearing this story. His dark, bushy eyebrows squeezed together, giving him an irritated look, accentuating frown lines that marred not just face, but his personality. Why had I not seen this sooner? Why had I thought he was still an attractive man?

I looked at Larry. "So, that was the end of it?" I asked. "As far as the photos went?"

Larry shook his head. "No. They threatened to put them on the Internet." He expelled a deep breath. "I've paid them twice."

My stomach clenched. It was one thing to know Bryan had been physical with Beverly, but what exactly did that mean? Had he been Monica Lewinsky physical? Physical enough for someone to have snapped a photo and manipulated it in a depraved way? I stopped this flow of thoughts when my kids, my mother, and his parents flashed in my head. It was unimaginable.

"Shouldn't you go to the police?" Toni said.

"That's what my wife Anna thinks. The blackmailer said if I go to the police, the pictures get released. If that happens, I'm ruined. I'm a veterinarian. People won't trust me anymore."

His gaze fixed on something outside the window. "I'd do anything to protect my family," he said. "I'm praying that with Beverly Foster's death, this is over."

His phone chimed. He had a look, reached into his pocket, and threw a twenty-dollar bill on the table. "I gotta go. Hope your husband doesn't find himself in my position. At least now, you've been warned."

I didn't feel grateful for the warning. "Thank you for your honesty, Larry. Good luck to you and Anna."

When Larry was gone, Toni shifted to the opposite side of the booth. "Oh, Quinn. You don't think Bryan..."

"It's clear to me now that he risked more than our marriage with this indiscretion." I pierced the top of his head with my gaze. He must have sensed my bitterness because he looked up, saw me, then looked away as if I was a stranger.

I'd lived with that man for nearly three decades.

"What do you think Larry meant when he said he'd do anything to protect his family?" Toni said. "Do you think he could have murdered Beverly?"

It was startling to think we'd been talking to a murderer. "I guess he has a pretty good motive. The police must have questioned him."

"I suppose so," Toni said. "Are you going to tell Bryan what Larry said?"

"Yes," I answered, surprisingly quick. "He should know." There'd be satisfaction in sharing this burden with the man who'd caused it. "Let's pay the bill and get out of here." I needed to get my mind on something less disturbing.

"Okay. Do you want to walk down to Break Thyme?" Toni asked. "You can show me the progress you've made over the last couple of weeks."

"I would love to do that." I also loved that Toni didn't mention the tree. I needed to focus on my café. On my opening. On positive things. No matter what happened, I'd rather die than give Bryan the satisfaction of seeing me fail.

I planned to walk past his table and out the door without looking at him, but when a family, who'd been blocking the way, moved toward the exit, I saw that he'd already left. Without a word.

Chapter Sixteen

IT WAS TIME FOR me to move on and focus my attention on my café. If I was going to be living on my own, this business would be my livelihood. Its success felt more important than ever to me, now.

But this nightmare with Bryan and his murdered mistress and photos, if they existed and became public, could ruin everything.

I pictured every single towns person walking straight past my café with eyes averted, never stepping inside, not knowing how to face me. *Poor Quinn, her husband had an affair with that murdered woman. There were photos! The police never found the killer. Do you think Bryan did it? Do you think it was Quinn?*

Good grief. I shivered at the thought.

Okay, calm down. I was envisioning the worst-case scenario, and while it was making me hyperventilate, I'd learned from my mother to prepare for the worst. When you do that, you're more than ready to face what's coming.

I knew one thing for sure, if a blackmailer threatened me, I'd go to the police. With that decision made, I had to be sure everything was on track for opening day.

After I'd given Toni a tour of my café-in-progress, we parted. I went home to do some marketing. With my designer, we'd brainstormed ideas of things to post on Break-Thyme's Facebook page, but I still had to figure out how that worked. I could hire someone to do this, but I was a bit of a control freak and wanted the voice of my café to be genuine.

"Are you ready?" Beverly's voice from behind scared the bejeezus out of me. This time, I recovered quickly as the phantom drifted into view.

"You did that on purpose, didn't you?" I said.

In Beverly's coy smile, I saw the truth in that. She could appear whenever and wherever she chose. I had a disturbing vision of having to manage her ghostly intrusions for the rest of my life. Someone was bound to see me "talking to myself." If I didn't want people to think I was demented, I needed to end this relationship.

"You've had a few days to absorb the change your life has taken," she said.

"Oh, I've been doing more than absorbing change. I had an enlightening conversation with Larry Lewis today. Remember him?"

"I do," she said, then shook her head wearily. "Larry can't let go of a fantasy he created after we spent an afternoon together on his boat."

Nothing about her appearance said sailor. The dress she wore looked expensive, and she didn't get those stilettos in Bookend Bay. Her delicate necklace and earrings looked like precious stones. Manicured nails, not a hair out of place. "You were going to buy a boat, huh?"

"Sure. Why not? Boating was one of my favorite childhood memories."

"I thought you grew up in West Virginia."

"We vacationed by the sea."

I shook my head. She had an answer for everything, likely lies. "So, you expect me to believe you had nothing to do with blackmailing Larry Lewis with indecent photos. Coincidentally, he'd been to a storage unit, too."

She blinked, then looked me in the eye. "I did not send him photos. Did he show them to you?"

"No, and I can imagine why not. He said someone doctored the pictures to make him look perverse."

Beverly looked surprised. "I know nothing about that. As I said, the man is delusional."

"But you had an affair with Larry?"

"I've already answered that. Larry is an attention seeker who likes to talk about his sexual fantasies. Why would he admit such a thing about himself otherwise? To a stranger, no less."

Either Beverly or Larry was lying, and my bet was on her. I thought back to the conversation with Larry. He'd not said Beverly was in the photos. This was implied, though, as far as I was concerned.

"Now, *if* nasty photos of Bryan got out, well, I can't imagine that would be good for your new café, Quinn. You could go out of business before you get your feet off the ground."

Good grief. Since I'd refused to help her, was she now going to try to sink my café? "Are you threatening my café? Did you topple that oak tree branch into my window?"

She tilted her head and looked at me as if I should know better. "I could say yes, and you wouldn't know the difference, but no, I didn't do it. I'm not that powerful, Quinn. I don't want to see your café fail. I want us to help each other."

That sure sounded like a threat, and the way she emphasized the word I made me think she and Bryan had talked about my café flopping. I didn't know how "powerful" she was, but she might know things that could hurt my family and possibly Break Thyme. I couldn't let that happen. "Are there photos of Bryan, like there were of Larry?"

"You deserve the answer to that question, Quinn, and I want to do whatever I can to help you resolve everything. When you've helped me."

Reasoning with Beverly was fruitless. I had to protect myself. "I don't trust you, Beverly, but I'll tell you what. You said you wanted me to retrieve a set of keys and give them to Hannah Wyatt. As a show of good faith, I'll get the keys. When you give me the evidence, I'll give the keys to Hannah."

She didn't hesitate. "1833 Lakeside Lane. My house. The keys are hidden in the rock garden out back. They're in a pill bottle glued to the underside of a piece of granite beside the pond. The rock has pink streaks and lilies planted beside it. I'll see you again when you have the keys."

Chapter Seventeen

TONI CALLED TO SAY she'd spoken to Colleen, and if I was available, she had time now to talk about the paranormal turn my life had taken. I needed all the help I could get, so I said let's go.

The door chimed as Toni and I entered Mystic Garden. I'd always considered Colleen's shop to be fun—for other people. Pagan-like people who believed in druids, astrology, Wicca, fairies, or ghosts. Not objective people like me, rooted in the sensible, but polar opposite of scientific study. Boy, was I wrong.

"It always smells so good in here," Toni said and leaned over a diffuser to breathe in the humid air. "I love jasmine."

A wooden shelf displayed a variety of diffusers. I picked up one that looked like a lotus flower. "My daughter would like this."

"You can give it to Samantha for her birthday next month," Toni said.

"Good idea. I'll grab it on our way out." There was so much to see in this store. My gaze bounced over wishing fountains, jewelry, dream catchers, lotions, mirrors, rune stones, books, and fluffy pillows with green eyes. Oh, that was Ginger, the resident cat. I gave her head a scratch, then made my way to the back of the store where Colleen Walsh, owner of Mystic Garden, was standing with her hands on her voluptuous hips. "Yes, lovie, that's perfect. Right there."

A teenage boy set down an ancient-looking trunk. Colleen smiled brightly when she saw Toni and me heading her way.

She turned her attention back to the boy. "Would you please unpack the prayer boxes and arrange them on the trunk?"

He gave her a quick nod. "I sure will."

"Thank you. You are a gem," she said.

Colleen greeted us with open arms and a warm hug. Her shaggy red curls tickled my nose. "I have tea steeping upstairs for us. I can't wait to hear all about your new acquaintance, Quinn."

I laughed. "The spirited swindler, you mean."

We followed Colleen upstairs, where she had a shabby chic sitting room. "This is cozy," I said. Pale pink curtains filtered the light from a large front window. Pillows adorned an ivory couch and coral and mint-striped armchairs. A large feathery flower arrangement sat on a side table. A tray with a lit candle, teapot, mugs, and a plate with slices of coffee cake sat on an upholstered stool serving as a coffee table. The pastel rag rug looked homemade. Light and airy, the atmosphere was what I hoped to attain in my Cozy Nook.

Colleen leaned down to pour tea. "Quinn, I heard the terrible news about your café window. Is it going to set you back very far?"

"I don't know yet. I have a wonderful contractor, so hopefully he'll have me back on track soon. He got the tree branch removed and boarded up the window for now." I slipped my cardigan off and set it over the arm of the sofa before sitting down. Lately, my body temperature fluctuated, and I was growing warm.

"Toni told me you've had a...visitor?" Colleen asked.

"Did she tell you my visitor is the ghost of the woman who was sleeping with my husband?"

Colleen froze in mid-pour. "Oh, lovie, you've got to be kidding. I'm sorry to hear that."

I didn't know Colleen well, yet it seemed we'd been friends forever. Some people were like that, you clicked quickly. "It's okay. Well, not really, but I'm keeping busy. I know I'll get through this one way or another."

"Yes, you will. You're a strong woman—you always have been." Colleen passed a mug to Toni. "Help yourself to the milk and lemon and honey."

I appreciated her faith in me and wondered why she talked like we had a history together.

She poured the tea. "Have you always seen ghosts?"

"Thanks, Colleen," said Toni. "Quinn hasn't so much spoken the word ghost, let alone seen one. She's the last person I'd ever expect to have a visitor from the dead."

"Toni's right," I said. "At first, I didn't know the woman was a ghost. I thought she was sick."

"You didn't tell me that," said Toni.

"Oh, yeah. She's pale all right. I think it's getting worse."

"So, this ghost..." said Colleen.

"Her name is Beverly," I added.

Colleen dropped into the chair across from Toni and me on the couch. She smoothed her ruffled cotton skirt." "So, Beverly admitted she was...intimate with your husband?"

"Well, not exactly, but he pretty much did. I asked her for details and all she would say was Bryan is corruptible."

"Corruptible? In what way?" Colleen asked.

"I have no idea, but it does concern me that this corruption could be linked to her murder. Did Toni tell you I had to give my cheating husband an alibi, so he didn't get charged with his lover's murder?"

Colleen's green eyes grew wide. "Nope, I would have remembered that detail."

Toni gave a clipped laugh. "I didn't know how much you wanted to share."

"I might as well let it all hang out. I mean with Colleen—not anyone else, please."

"Thanks for clarifying," Toni said, dryly.

"In all my years, I've never heard anything like this," Colleen said. "Your story takes the cake." She lifted the plate of cake, offering.

We all laughed, and I was grateful for it. If I couldn't laugh at this craziness, I'd lose my mind.

"The problem is Beverly has threatened to send evil spirits my way if I don't do what she wants. Do you think that's possible? Could she have had anything to do with that tree falling on my café?"

"Honestly, I don't know. People who believe their homes are haunted complain of slamming doors, window shades flying up, lights turning on and off. Some say their objects are haunted—making them cold, or anxious, or giving them strange dreams."

I thought about the breakfast platter I'd found in my fridge. "Do ghosts ever do useful things?"

"Oh, sure they do, although it's not a commonly held belief in the Western world. For instance, Russians have their *domovye*."

"Domo-who?" Toni asked.

"Ghosts that help with chores," Colleen said. "It's mainly *our* culture who believe the dead only come back to address their grievances."

"Where do I sign up for the ghost that cleans toilets?" said Toni.

"Sure, *you* get clean toilets and I get a vindictive mistress," I said, sourly.

Toni patted my knee.

"I think it's a coincidence the tree fell," said Colleen. "But if Beverly catches wind of it, she might claim she brought it down, just to further intimidate you."

I'd planned to tell them about my promise to retrieve Beverly's keys. But I changed my mind. Toni would insist on coming with me, which meant she'd have to take more time off work. If I was going to do this, and I wasn't one-hundred percent sure, it would be during the day when I could see what I was doing.

"This is excellent tea." Toni put her mug on the tray. "Don't you think it's strange that suddenly Quinn can see ghosts?"

"Ghost," I clarified, not wanting to tempt the undead. "One ghost. I'm not welcoming any more into my life."

"I was going to ask about that," said Colleen. "And by the way, the tea is ginger, turmeric—"

A bang sounded, making me jump. I looked to see a picture had fallen off the wall.

Colleen jumped up. "Oh, dear," she said, bending down to pick it up.

"Did it break?" Toni leaned forward to see.

"Clean in two." Colleen held up two halves of a broken framed watercolor of a bear. "It split right between the eyes."

"What a shame," I said.

"It was from a spirit animal collection I was selling last year. I would have given it away, but I didn't know any Virgos."

"Quinn is a Virgo," said Toni.

Colleen looked down at the two pieces in her hands. "You don't see your ghost here now, do you?"

"No," I said, feeling especially creeped out. "Do you think it's a message meant for me?"

"I'd say so," said Toni. "But then I have an exasperating habit of looking for meaning in everything."

Colleen set the pieces down on the floor, leaning them against the wall. "The bear has several meanings, primarily it's a sign of strength, confidence, and standing against adversity."

"Quinn, that's you to a tee, especially these days," Toni said.

"The bear is also a sign you need to take time for yourself, time to heal," Colleen said.

That all sounded lovely, but I couldn't take this too seriously. "I'll take time to heal when I've succeeded in my stand against adversity."

Toni squeezed my shoulder. "You're not alone in this."

"I'm here to help, too," said Colleen. "Can I share something with you both? It's just come to me."

I hoped it was good news—like more cake or something else sugar-laden. "Sure. Please do."

"Quinn, we've both lived in Bookend Bay a long time, but we've not gotten to know each other beyond saying our hellos."

Probably because I'd rarely been in her shop, and Colleen didn't have children, so we'd not run in the same circles.

"Do you know anything about auras?" she asked.

I was taken aback by this since it was the second time that week someone had spoken to me about auras. It wasn't something that had ever come up before. "Not really, no."

"They're believed to be an electromagnetic energy field that every living thing emits." Colleen smiled softly. "Your aura has changed and not in the usual way—everyone's energy changes over time. It's not that. I've been seeing people's auras for so long, I don't think too much about them, but yours stands out."

"Okay, well, you're not the first person to mention this." I told Colleen and Toni what Beverly said about me having two auras.

"Ah, that's a good way to describe it. There are several colors in a person's aura, but I've not seen one like yours. You have a unique, additional aura that trails after you."

"Do you think this makes me attractive to ghosts?"

Colleen gave a soft snort. "I suppose it might, but I honestly don't know what it means. I'll do some research, and if I learn anything of value, I'll let you know."

"Thank you, Colleen. I have to get going as soon as I buy one of your lotus diffusers."

I wasn't sure why, but I felt better having talked to Colleen and Toni. With these women, I felt loved and supported. I could share all the details of my screwed-up life and be met with compassion, understanding, and continued friendship. I wasn't alone in this, and that erased my jitters.

But it also filled me with that sadness again. This was what my marriage should feel like.

Chapter Eighteen

Before I went home, I drove to 1833 Lakeside Lane to see what kind of house Beverly had lived in. Silver Leaf Estates was one of the more affluent communities along the shore of Lake Superior. Between the sprawling lakefront properties, I caught glimpses of navy water, darkening as the sun set.

Slowly, I drove by Beverly's stunning beach house, a sleek, modern two-story with expansive windows. Who knew impersonating grieving family members could be so lucrative?

No car in the driveway and no lights inside the house. Since she'd not indicated otherwise, I assumed Beverly had lived alone, but I certainly couldn't be sure. I considered sneaking into her garden now. The neighboring houses were probably seventy feet apart, but second-story windows would provide a clear view of Beverly's back yard. What possible reason could I have for creeping around in the dark?

I turned my truck around and went home.

The next morning, I was prepared. I'd decided on a cover story in case a neighbor saw me in the garden. I'd pretend to be a potential vacation property renter who'd gotten the address wrong. I was just scoping out the yard to see if it was safe for my grandson since our family planned to rent the home later that summer.

It was a gloomy day with not a sliver of blue sky. The forecast called for rain after noon, so I had to get moving. Once again, I drove through the gates of Silver Leaf Estates and parked my truck across the road from 1833 Lakeside Lane.

With my phone in hand, I pretended to be researching this potential rental. Peeking over the screen, I scanned the neighbor's houses. Everything was quiet. Beverly's house looked as lifeless as it had last night. If anyone was watching, I'd look suspicious if I sat any longer.

Just do it!

I grabbed my purse, got out of the truck, and crossed the street. Keeping an eye out for signs of life, I headed up the driveway. A flagstone path led around to the backyard. As I followed it, I looked around. No gate barred the entrance to the back of the house.

Wow, I thought, as I turned the corner. What a view. The yard was beautifully landscaped around a pool, deck, and outdoor kitchen, but the showstopper was the lake, although it looked rough at the moment with whitecaps crashing into the shore.

The wind was growing stronger, rustling leaves overhead. I pushed my hair back, tucking strands behind my ears as I looked for the pond Beverly had mentioned. On the other side of the patio, I saw cattails standing tall. That must be it.

I hurried across the patio to the short path leading to the pond, eyes peeled for granite.

When Beverly said the rock had pink streaks, a picture had formed in my mind. From beside the pond, I looked clockwise through the garden for lilies. A stand of tiger lilies, not yet in bloom, was at eleven o'clock. I had to step into the garden to get to them.

This was where my rental story could fall apart if I was caught. I cast a glance at the neighbor's house. Everything was still, but with the sounds of the lake and the wind, I probably wouldn't hear anyone if they came up behind me.

Oh man, I didn't want to do this.

Biting back trepidation, I treaded softly to the lilies. I didn't see any pink-streaked rocks. A huge, pinkish-colored boulder, that I couldn't possibly nudge, sat beside a salt and pepper rock. That couldn't be it.

Perspiration broke out on my forehead at my hairline. I used the toe of my shoe to lift a leafy fern growing beside the lilies. Nothing.

Gingerly, I stepped to the other side of the lilies, where smaller rocks were hidden under Creeping Phlox.

My heart picked up when I saw a mottled pinkish-red and grey-black rock. I squatted and used both hands, meaning to roll the stone from its bed.

It wasn't easy. The thing was planted solidly. Why didn't I stick a trowel in my purse?

I had to use my fingers to dig away some of the earth covering part of the stone. It seemed to take forever. I had to stop to wipe droplets out of my eyes. These rushes of heat were happening more and more.

Finally, I got the stone up and thanked my lucky stars when I saw a pill bottle glued to the underside of the rock, just like Beverly had said.

A seagull squawked overhead, giving me a start. My chest rose and fell rapidly, like I'd been running for my life.

Hurry up!

I got the bottle open and turned it upside down, letting the keys fall into my hand. They were small. I couldn't imagine what they unlocked. I shoved them in my pocket, stuffed the bottle into the earth, and dropped the rock on top.

Looking down, I noticed a green stain on my khaki pants at the knee. I didn't even remember kneeling.

As I brushed the dirt from my hands, I was breathing hard. I made myself slow down to a saunter.

Everything is okay. You did it!

Relief washed over me as I left the backyard, rounded the house, and started to cut across the lawn.

Then, I heard a door opening—the front door of Beverly's house!

I froze.

A woman came out and hurried down the steps toward me. A bit younger than me, her expression was not friendly.

I swallowed hard, aware of the dirt embedded in my fingers and my stained pants.

"What are you doing?" she demanded.

Chapter Nineteen

I ALMOST HELD OUT my hand in greeting before remembering the filth. "Wha—hello!" I said as my mind scrambled,
then scrambled some more. Had she seen me digging
through the garden with my bare hands? I couldn't say
I was thinking of renting the place. What reason would I
have for overturning rocks?

"Can I help you with something?" she said.

"Yes, thank you. I'm looking for Beverly Foster."

She pulled her emerald sweater closed and hugged
herself. "Beverly died a few days ago."

"Oh no," I said. "I'm so very sorry."

The dark-haired woman was younger than Beverly. I
wondered if this was Hannah Wyatt. I looked for physical
resemblances to see if they might be related. It was hard
to tell. Perhaps the woman had come to look after the
house—water plants, pick up mail, that sort of thing.

"Why are you looking for her?" she asked.

That was a good question, especially if she'd seen me
digging in the garden. "I didn't really know Beverly." I
reached over and pinched off a dead leaf from a holly

bush. "She was thinking of hiring me to look after the gardens. I said I'd come over and have a look."

Her eyes widened. "She did? That's odd. She didn't mention it to me. I like gardening. I've never complained about it."

Okay, so it looked like this woman lived there, too. "Oh, well, we didn't get into details. Maybe it was a surprise?"

"Not a welcome one. I don't know why she'd think we should pay a gardener to do what we can do ourselves. But that's Beverly." She cut herself off. "That *was* Beverly. I won't be needing your services."

I tried to look disappointed. "That's okay. I understand." Actually, I understood very little, like why didn't Beverly mention someone else lived in this house? I couldn't waste this opportunity to learn more. "Beverly and I met at a funeral. That's where we got to talking about landscaping and her gardens. She said nothing about you." I hoped I wasn't digging too deep into her relationship with Beverly and making her any more suspicious than she might be.

"That's strange, considering it's my house."

"Oh," I said. "That is a rather important piece of information."

"Yes, but I always told her to think of this as her home, too. She'd recently moved in." Her eyes grew moist. "I don't know what I'm going to do without her."

I was beginning to get the picture. Beverly and this woman were in a loving relationship. I wondered how that hunk of granite become so embedded if Beverly had only recently moved in.

"I'm sorry for your loss. It must be hard to imagine your future without her. I know what that's like." I tried not to think of myself as being manipulative. I *could* relate to unforeseen changes in relationships.

"I'm Danielle." She twisted a ring on her finger, then held it out for me to see. The stone was dark blue, set in a gold knot. I knew little about gemstones, but this one was big, probably near four carats if it was real.

"It's nice to meet you." I didn't want to tell her my name. "That's a beautiful ring."

"Beverly gave it to me the night before she was killed. It's a sapphire. It was meant as a promise, a commitment to our spending our lives together. We planned to marry next year."

"She was killed?" I hoped I sounded sincerely surprised.

Danielle sniffed. "Yes—savagely. Shot in the back. I just can't understand it."

I touched my hand to my mouth. "That's horrible. Have they found her killer?"

She shook her head. "I don't know what to think. Beverly might have had a secret side to her, from where her body was found, that is."

"Oh? Where was that?"

"A swinger's club. It just doesn't add up. I'm sorry. I don't know why I'm telling you this."

It was nothing more than what was in the news. "Don't apologize. It helps to talk about these things. Probably easier to talk to a stranger."

Danielle rubbed her arm. A sea of clouds darkened the sky. "You're right. I—I'd not been honest with my family or friends as to the nature of my relationship with Beverly. I was married to a man for many years. Beverly was my first... No one knows how broken I am over this." She seemed to catch her breath. "I apologize again for dumping on you."

"It's okay. Really." I meant it. I felt for Danielle and hated when people couldn't be honest about who they were and who they loved. How could you live like that? I'd never understood why people thought they had the right to judge another person's sexual orientation.

She wiped her eyes. "So, what do you think of my gardens? Horribly in need of a good weeding?"

"No, no. You have a beautiful home."

"Thank you. I worked my butt off for it. I own Feathers & Co."

"Really? That's you? I buy your bras. They're so comfortable. I can't stand to wear under-wire any longer."

We were getting off-track, but it seemed I was doing Danielle some good. I liked her, quite a bit more than Beverly, which made me wonder what Danielle was doing with a woman like the swindler.

Then I realized a terrible possibility. What if the keys didn't belong to Beverly at all? What if I'd just stolen Danielle's keys? How did I know Beverly was the one who'd hidden them under a rock? My stomach turned over at my foolishness. Beverly had called this *her* house, but how credible was that?

As the owner of Feathers & Co., Danielle was likely a wealthy woman. Beverly's target? Danielle hadn't questioned my poor excuse for traipsing through her property. Maybe she was too trusting, and this made her an easy target. If what Larry said was true, then Danielle was better off without Beverly. Why did she want these keys given to another woman and not to Danielle? And who was Hannah Wyatt to Beverly—another lover?

As my mind raced, Danielle had been talking about under-wire bras causing headaches and neck pain. I nodded. And rib pain, too, right under the arm.

Danielle continued. "Beverly and I had much in common. That was why we got on so well. She worked independently, so she understood and supported my business."

"That sounds ideal," I said, supposing she meant Beverly's professional mourning business.

"Bev was going to flip houses. Buy rundown places and renovate them."

What? When was she going to fit that in? Renovator, fake griever, husband seducer, blackmailer—it seemed like a handful for one person. "Funny, I can't picture Beverly in a hardhat." Danielle must not know that Beverly had absconded with Andrew Hill's deposits.

"She was putting together a team," said Danielle, wiping a tear from her eye. "I'd just written her a check for a hundred thousand dollars, then she was killed."

"Oh no. I hope she didn't cash it."

She shrugged, like that kind of money wasn't significant to her. Leaves scuttled across the stone walkway.

Danielle shivered. "I've just gone on and on, blabbing all sorts of personal stuff to a—a very nice stranger. Believe me, I'm not myself. I should get back inside before I subject you to my home movies."

I smiled. "Please don't worry about it. We need to talk about these things, right?"

"I suppose so. I'll let you get on with your day. You must have many gardens to look after."

"I sure do. It was nice to meet you." The keys I'd stolen from her yard were burning a hole in my pocket, so I said goodbye.

I was happy to get back in my truck and leave Lakeside Lane behind. I couldn't wait for the swindler to make an appearance—I had many questions for Beverly Foster. And until she answered them, I would not tell her I'd found her keys.

Chapter Twenty

THE NEXT DAY, I stood at Break Thyme in the Cozy Nook, frowning at the damaged wall after hanging up the phone with my insurance company.

Focus on the good news.

The structural damage to the building from the fallen tree limb was minor and would be covered by my property owner. The windows would be replaced. The mess inside was a different story. I would have to cover it. Thankfully, it wasn't extensive. With a shop vac and good wash, I'd returned the room to its pre-calamity state.

The real problem was timing. The windows had been a custom order—they'd taken six weeks to build and install. My café was slated to open in three.

Where there'd been a wall of light and a sea of blue, there was now plywood. It cast the whole café in shadow. There was no hiding the ugly boards.

The reason I'd expanded my café into the Cozy Nook was to make the café special by bringing in more light and giving my customers a view of the lake. I cringed at the thought of my customers arriving to see a boarded-up wall. I only had one opportunity to make a first impression.

As I walked up the two steps into the main café, details swarmed my mind. An electrician was coming tomorrow. Furniture was arriving early next week. My new head barista, Poppy, was coming in today to get acquainted.

I'd liked Poppy right away. No one I'd interviewed had her experience. Unfortunately, I could only count on her until September when she'd go back to college.

Before our meeting, I needed to tidy myself up and change out of my old jeans and sweatshirt. I had another thirty minutes—enough time to bring in the paint for the bathroom. Instead of a full remodel, I'd updated the fixtures and would have a new mirror installed.

Someone banged on the front door. Shoot, was it Poppy already? Through the window, I could see a woman standing outside. Not Poppy. She turned her head as if she were speaking to someone behind her.

I brushed dust from my clothes and opened the door. "Hello," I said to the brunette. Behind her stood a guy with a camera. "Can I help you?"

"You're Quinn Delaney?" she asked.

"I am."

The woman extended her hand. "Hi. I'm Millie. We spoke on the phone. I'm from the Bugle. We're here to do your interview." The Bugle was our local newspaper.

"That's not today," I said. It hadn't been on my schedule.

Brown eyes, behind over-sized glasses, squinted at me. "It's definitely today." Her gaze swept me quickly from top to bottom. Besides my dusty apparel, I wore no makeup and my hair—well, I'd had better hair days.

"I can't do this today," I said, hearing the alarm in my voice. "I had a tree crash through the window. The place is a mess." This wasn't exactly true, but I didn't want any photos showing boarded-up windows.

"Oh gosh. That's horrible. I hope you weren't hurt."

"No. No one was hurt."

She rolled her upper lip thoughtfully. "I'm sorry about the tree, but we're going to have to do this today. We're on a tight schedule."

The Bookend Bay Bugle was on a tight schedule? Must be the stream of newsworthy happenings about town. I guessed it had been a big week for the paper, considering Beverly's death. I was thankful Bryan's name hadn't been linked to the murder—not yet. Worry for my business crept up again.

I didn't want to sound ungrateful for the newspaper's promotion. "Okay. I do appreciate you covering my café." I had my fingers crossed for an overwhelming turnout on opening day. I planned to give a Rosemary Thyme Scone to the first 100 customers, and this article would help get that message out. Even in this day of online news, The Bugle was beloved in the community.

"Why don't we take our photo here?" Millie said. "We'll get this beautiful sign. This is a new color on the door, isn't it? It sure gives a welcoming feeling."

That was a good idea, and I appreciated the compliment. I loved the marine blue door. "Thank you, Millie.

That will work. Can you give me ten minutes to clean up? This tree thing has thrown me for a loop."

"Yes, of course."

I quickly changed my clothes, but belatedly realized I had no mirror to apply makeup other than the tiny one in my blush compact. I had to do my best with that. I pulled the elastic from my hair, brushed, and fluffed with my fingers, angling the mirror to no avail. Oh well, this would have to do.

Out front, Millie was directing the camera guy. He changed position and snapped a photo of Courtesy Boulevard, then he relaxed. "Got it," he said.

"Good." Millie looked at me. I saw a slight frown in her expression, quickly replaced by a smile. "Let's take a couple of photos first and then we'll do the interview."

Down the street, I saw Oliver standing outside his store looking my way. I hoped the town know-it-all wouldn't come over to give me expert tips. "I'm ready," I said, trying to muster excitement. This wasn't how I'd pictured the weeks leading up to opening day, juggling a conniving, blackmailing ghost; an absent, cheating spouse, and the possibility I was being considered a suspect in a murder. Oh, and dare I forget the tree branch through my windows.

"You're sure you're ready? Okay then. You're in a good position right there." As Millie turned to the camera guy, I saw Poppy zipping across the street toward us. She waved, and I smiled back, feeling strangely at ease at the sight of her. The bright orange blazer she wore looked great. With skin that seemed to glow naturally, she had a girl-next-door prettiness. I figured her beauty went farther than skin deep.

"Quinn? Over here," Millie said as if she were speaking to a four-year-old.

"One of my employees has just arrived." I wondered if I should include her in the photo but then thought that wasn't fair to pounce on her.

"This looks exciting," Poppy skipped up onto the sidewalk a few feet behind Millie.

"A little publicity for the café," I said. "I'm sorry, Poppy, are you able to wait until we finish this for our chat?"

"Sure, I can." Her gaze moved to my hair. "Er, Quinn, you have a bump. Do you mind..." She stepped forward and patted my head, then smoothed it down further. "There. That's better."

So that's why Millie was frowning at me. I wished she'd said something. "Thank you, Poppy. I appreciate that. I want to make a good impression."

"Can I make a suggestion?"

Millie let out her breath in a huff.

"Of course," I said.

"If you turn just a little and they shoot you from where I'm standing, you'll have that gorgeous flower planter in the background as well as your lovely café sign."

I looked behind me. "She's right," I said to Millie. "Can we do that?"

"Sure," the camera guy said, moving into position.

"Are we ready?" Millie asked impatiently.

"Yes." I gave her my warmest smile. "Thank you for your patience, Millie. It makes a big difference to work with positive people." I smiled at Poppy, feeling a boost of energy from this young woman. I don't think I could have made a better choice in my head barista.

The interview for The Bugle went well. The next morning, I learned the article would be in tomorrow's paper. This news helped perk me up after learning about the window replacement delays.

Poppy had a suggestion to pretty up the boarded wall. She recommended I buy porthole decals to place across the boards to make it look like the café was inside a ship. Or in keeping with my herbal theme, I might find potted herb decals. Poppy even offered to stop in at our local art shop for suggestions.

I was lucky to have found her and told her so.

Beverly's absence weighed on me. She said she'd be back when I got the keys, yet a whole day had gone by. Did I dare presume she'd given up the ghost and had vamoosed to the afterlife forever? It seemed a little too good to be true.

There was one thing I shouldn't put off any longer. As much as I wanted to avoid an uncomfortable conversation with Bryan, I picked up my phone and called him. The phone rang five times before he answered.

"Hello, Quinn. Listen, I'm sorry I didn't speak to you at the Black Cap. You looked busy and my presence was likely...awkward."

I supposed that was true. "You could have called, Bryan. It's been nearly a week." I wondered if he'd tell me he was looking into traveling to the Far East. If he was planning this, hoping to repair our marriage, I wondered if he'd considered the timing. A trip that far that would take me away from my new café could ensure my failure.

"I know," he said. "I'm feeling a lot of shame about this. I can't face you right now. You didn't tell the kids, did you?"

That was a weak excuse, and of course I didn't tell the kids. *Man up, Bryan.* "No." I waited for him to ask about how I was managing in the wake of his indiscretion.

He said nothing, and the silence felt terribly awkward. Well, if he had nothing to say, I sure did. He needed to know what had happened to Larry Lewis.

"I have something to tell you," I said. When I finished the gruesome details, the line was so silent I wondered if we'd been disconnected. "Bryan?"

"I—I'm here. How did you find this guy?" I told him about calling his dead colleague's wife Ruth and how she led me to the funeral home.

"You've been busy." He said it like I'd done something wrong. "You shouldn't be getting involved in this."

"Your mistress is dead. Murdered. The police asked me to provide your alibi. I'm already involved. Do we have to be concerned about receiving a package like Larry did?" It was a question I never could have imagined asking.

"No. I don't see how there could be anything like that. I told you—things didn't go that far."

"Because she was murdered."

He was quiet.

"I've got to go now. I've got a lot to do." If he cared about me, this would be the moment to ask about the café.

"Quinn?"

I waited.

"I'm sorry. Really, I am."

That was it? Sorry was too easy right now, and I didn't want to give him the chance to talk about him coming home. I wasn't ready for that.

"Goodbye, Bryan." I disconnected, surprised by how strong I felt. I remembered what Colleen said about my ability to stand against adversity. I would get through this. Even though I was no further to the truth about Beverly, my heart was recovering. I didn't need a spirit bear to tell me how to heal. I knew what I had to do to get through this, and I knew how I was going to get started.

Chapter Twenty-One

My recovery plan was going to start with friendship and chocolate.

It was late Friday afternoon, and Toni had invited me to dinner. On my way home to freshen up and check on Oreo, I stopped at Henrietta's Bakery and bought dessert for Toni and me—Molten Chocolate Lava Cake, Bittersweet Chocolate Tart, and a Caramel Pecan Skillet Brownie.

Oreo greeted me at the door. Like all Maine Coons, he was friendly, curious, and always happy to see his humans. I bent to pat his head and scratch behind his ears. While I removed my shoes, he got up on his hind legs to check out the box of dessert I'd set on the table by the front door.

"No, no, no. Not for you. Come in the kitchen, and I'll get you a treat." He padded along behind me, making a soft chirping sound in support of this routine.

Once he'd had his treats, I sat on the window seat, his favorite place in the house. Bounding up beside me, he swept his head against my shoulder. I grabbed the cat brush and gave him a good going over. He loved a good

A SPIRITED SWINDLER

brushing and lifted his head so I could get under his chin. When I was done, he arched his back and stepped into my lap.

"Oh no, you don't," I complained as he kneaded my thighs with his claws. His thick tail bopped me in the face.

"Pfft." I picked a hair from my lip. He settled down, and as he rested his head on my knees, I tried to still my thoughts as I resumed petting.

Every time an upsetting thought popped into my head, I noticed it, but then I let it go. I felt anger, sadness, and shame rise in me. I didn't stop these unpleasant feelings and eventually they dissipated—at least for now. This was a technique Toni and I had started practicing. For me, it had been a lifesaver since I'd acquired Break Thyme. Just because the café was my dream come true didn't mean it hadn't been stressful.

My phone rang, interrupting my small moment of peace. "Sorry, buddy." I shuffled him to the cushion and retrieved my phone. The screen displayed a phone number I didn't recognize.

"Hello," I said.

"Hi, is this Quinn?" It was a male voice, vaguely familiar.

"It is."

"It's Larry Lewis. I hope I'm not catching you at a bad time."

"No, it's fine. What can I do for you?" I asked as I put a glass in the dishwasher.

"Good. I won't keep you long." Traffic thrummed in the background. "I don't have much time. I just wanted to warn you."

My body tensed. "Warn me about what?"

"It's not over. I received another blackmail letter. Whoever was working with Beverly is keeping it up."

Anger boiled inside me. Surely Beverly knew who this person was, yet she protected them by not revealing their identity.

"I'm sorry, Larry. This must be horrible for you. Do you not think it would be best to tell the police about this?"

"I don't know. If those photos get out, I'm ruined. It won't matter that they're fakes."

He was probably right about that, as unfair as it was. What a mess he was in, even if it was of his own doing. I thought of my mother and how she'd been victimized by that email scam. She'd done nothing wrong, yet it hadn't mattered. Even when warned against it, her friends still followed the scammers' instructions. By sending money, they'd just reinforced the scheme.

Everyone needed to be extra vigilant against these things. We were all vulnerable. Bryan was an intelligent person, yet he'd been as much a fool as Larry had been. Did we all have weaknesses that were ripe for exploitation? Did I?

Larry cleared his throat. "I don't want to ruin your day, but I thought you should know."

"I understand." The peace I'd acquired was blown to bits.

We said goodbye.

I was livid at Beverly. Livid at whoever she'd worked with. Livid that I'd been pulled into this.

Then a horrible thought occurred to me. Maybe Beverly's partner was Danielle. *Cripes!* Would she figure out I was Bryan's wife?

I slumped down onto my bed and held my head in my hands. *Why was this happening to me?*

After a few deep breaths, I remembered my daughter, at eighteen years old, begging for an answer to that question as she sobbed over a broken relationship. I'd told her these moments, as devastating as they are, are opportunities to learn and grow. It was painful, yes, but the ending of that relationship had given her the space for something new. Something better was coming. Better than she could imagine.

I sat there, struggling to take my own advice. My world was cracking and breaking and disintegrating around me, taking my insides and churning them into something unrecognizable.

Everything is over. I couldn't see how my marriage could survive—should survive. I couldn't see my future as I'd always envisioned it. I couldn't see myself alone.

You can't see the future because it's going to be better than you can ever imagine. I barely believed the optimistic thought that had popped into my head, but I was grateful for it. I repeated that mantra as I changed into leggings and a long-sleeved T-shirt. If I said it enough, it would start to feel true.

Last night, Toni and I had devoured too many of her fish tacos and mango salsa to eat all the dessert. Spending an evening with my friend pulled me out of the doldrums.

The next morning was sunny with periwinkle blue skies. Living this far north, I had a loose rule that mornings above sixty-eight degrees meant it was warm enough for coffee outside on the deck. I scooted out front to pick up my copy of the Bugle from where it lay on the driveway.

"Holy cow," I said under my breath. I'd gotten the front page. My photo turned out pretty good, considering I'd not been ready for it. Grateful for small blessings, I grabbed a fleece sweater, coffee, paper, and a half-brownie leftover from last night.

I held the door for Oreo as he sniffed the outside air. If everything was to his liking, he would hang out with me on the deck—that was as far as he would go. Apparently, all smelled well. He jumped up onto a patio chair and curled into a fluff ball.

The newspaper article was glowing. Considering the week I'd had, I was extra thankful. I flipped through the rest of the paper.

My job for that morning was to set up a Facebook Page for Break Thyme. I retrieved my laptop and got to work with limited success until the landline rang inside the house. I hardly answered that phone these days since it was usually telemarketers. I should change my message to say this is Quinn, I don't need my ducts cleaned. I let the phone go to voicemail.

The phone rang again. Sometimes an old friend or family member called on that line. Now, I had to know if that was the case. I went inside and answered the phone.

"Hello, Quinn Delaney," said a woman. "I saw the front page of the Bugle this morning."

After Larry's call yesterday, I was instantly on edge, not recognizing this voice. "Who is this?"

"It's Danielle Karhu. We met when you were creeping around my house looking for Beverly. It's remarkable you manage to work as a landscaper and as a café owner. You certainly are a busy woman."

Holy crow. I didn't know what to say. What did she want? Was she dangerous? Was she going to accuse me of stealing those keys? "I can explain, Danielle." I scrambled for a way to not tell her Beverly's ghost sent me to her house.

"Go ahead, because I'm considering calling the police. Someone murdered Beverly, after all."

I didn't want her to do that. She'd taken the time to find my home number instead of calling the police right away, so that was a good sign—as long as she wasn't Beverly's partner in crime. Would she threaten to call the police if she was?

A story formulated in my mind. Was I actually getting good at spewing falsehoods on the fly? "I didn't tell you the truth because...because it's hard for me to talk about." I wasn't sure Danielle would relate to this, considering she'd blurted her life story to a stranger.

"I think you owe me the truth," she said.

"Yes, I do. If you want to hear it, that is. You may not want your memory of Beverly tarnished."

"I need to know what was real." I heard the determination in her voice and understood the need to know the truth might be why she hadn't gone to the police. Maybe because she suspected Beverly of wrongdoing and wanted information.

"After Beverly was killed, my husband admitted he and Beverly had an affair. I...I found your address on his phone." That part wasn't true, but I couldn't tell her who gave me her address. I hoped she wouldn't question it.

Danielle let out a long breath. "I knew something was wrong. I suspected she was involved in...well, I didn't want to think it was an affair." She no longer sounded despondent. She was getting over Beverly's death, perhaps having learned a truth or two about her character. Maybe we could both learn something.

"It's more complicated than that," I said. "Do you want to know what else I've uncovered?" I said on a hunch.

She hesitated. Maybe she may want to keep her memories of Beverly as pure as she could? "Yes, I do," she said.

I told her about Larry and how he was being blackmailed with doctored photos. "It hasn't ended with Beverly's death. She was working with someone." I acted as if I suspected her of nothing, mainly because I was leaning this way.

"Who?" Danielle asked.

"I don't know that—not yet. I do know Beverly had a pattern of unprincipled behavior. I met her ex-husband.

He accused her of running off with his clients' deposits. It nearly ruined his reputation."

"You believed him?"

"I did. Yes." I almost slipped and said Beverly denied it of course.

"I believe him, too," she said. "I didn't tell you this, but days before her death, Beverly cashed the check I gave her, then she disappeared. She didn't return any of my calls."

Oreo sidled in through the open door, distracting me for a second. "Oh no. I'm sorry, Danielle. That was a lot of money."

"Yes, it was. Thankfully, the amount is not a loss that will change my life in any big way. I'm hurt, but it's the audacity of it that makes me angry. She lied to me, and I fell for it—not just about her fake business, but she said she wanted to spend the rest of our lives together. I believed that and now I feel stupid."

I could relate to that, and my mother's friends had felt the same way after they'd been scammed. "Beverly was a professional swindler. This was not your fault, and you are not stupid. I've read up on scams. Do you know how many intelligent people have been victims of fraud—heads of state, big investment companies, corporate attorneys, pension fund trustees, to name a few."

"Thank you, Quinn. You've been her victim, too, I suppose."

I still was. "Do you think we could meet for a coffee?" I asked. I *was* feeling inclined to believe Danielle. "Maybe if we put our heads together, we can figure out who

Beverly was working with. I'm worried she had photos of my husband."

"Yes," Danielle said without hesitation. "I'll meet you. You live in Bookend Bay?"

"Yes."

"There's an inn on the highway between us."

Good grief. Don't say The Blackwood Motor Inn where my husband may have conducted his affair.

"It's called Glen Erin. Do you know it?"

"Yes. Isn't it a Bed and Breakfast?"

"They have a dining room that's open to the public."

"Okay," I said. "I can be there in thirty minutes."

"Good. I have an idea who might be able to help us with this," she said.

I felt a sliver of hope. "That's great. I'll see you soon." I'd given her enough details that she'd not seemed to notice I didn't explain what I was doing at her house. Hopefully, I could keep it that way.

After I hung up the phone, I grabbed my laptop from outside. I sent a quick email to Poppy asking if she knew anything about Facebook. I had to face that I couldn't do everything myself. I offered to pay her extra for help with marketing.

Chapter Twenty-Two

I PULLED INTO THE parking lot of the Glen Erin B&B, a historic, three-level Victorian manor. The place looked deserted, except for a white van with a Bronson Bathroom Concepts logo.

As I approached the entrance, I heard construction—the high-pitched whine of a buzz-saw. This locale would not work for a chat over coffee.

As I was checking my watch, a car came into view on the highway. It slowed and pulled into the parking lot, coming to a stop beside my truck. I recognized Danielle behind the wheel.

"Hello," she said, closing her door behind her and joining me. "It's closed?"

"Yes. Looks like the B&B is getting new bathrooms. We could go for a walk along the road. It's not busy."

"Let's do that. I need to grab my hat from the car. I used to worship the sun, now I hide from it."

"I hear you. I'll get my hat, too. I've got sunscreen if you need some."

"Thanks, but I've already got it on." I'd also been a fan of tanning in my younger years and now wished I'd taken better care of my skin. It was frightening how little concern I'd had in my twenties for my future self.

Duly protected, shaded by wide brims, we headed across the parking lot.

Danielle looked over at the old manor. "I had my heart set on their Apple Cheese Danish, and they make excellent coffee here."

I'd developed a sweet tooth myself in the last couple of years. "I couldn't resist if it was apple and cheese."

"I know. Their cheese is the creamiest I've ever had."

"Now I want one, too," I said, stepping into stride beside Danielle, along the south shoulder of the highway.

"We'll have to meet again and satisfy our need for cheese," she said.

I laughed, remembering how much I'd like Danielle when I'd been breaking into her property. "I want to apologize again for misleading you. I froze. I didn't know what to say."

"It's okay, Quinn. I understand it was an awkward situation."

We passed a small tree where a red-winged blackbird gave a twilling call. "You said you knew someone who might help us get answers," I said.

"Yes. He was a friend of Beverly's. I hope he'll be of help, but I don't know if that's too optimistic."

"What do you mean?"

"I mean, I don't know if he's trustworthy. I don't know him well. He was the one who introduced me to Beverly."

So far, everyone was connected to Beverly through the funeral parlor. "Where did you meet him?" I asked.

"I met him at a marketing seminar. I rarely attend those things, but my assistant broke his leg and was in Emergency. The seminar was online, so he just forwarded a link to me. Once I got that going, they asked us to partner up with one of the other attendees. That's how I met Gunner."

"Gunner? The director from the funeral home?"

"Yes. You know him?"

"Not really, no," I said. "I spoke to him. That's how I found out about Larry, the man who is being blackmailed."

"Gunner told you about that?"

"No, he wasn't the one who brought it up," I said. "His associate told me about Larry. Gunner said Larry had a reputation for affairs, and he intended to soil Beverly's reputation for snubbing him."

"That sounds a bit like damage control. I can't imagine Gunner saying anything else. He wouldn't want a rumor like that to harm the funeral home's reputation."

"Right. That makes sense." I wouldn't broadcast it if someone accused my employee of blackmailing one of our customers. My first instinct would be disbelief and denial. I'd probably defend my employee as Gunner had done, especially if we had a good relationship.

Danielle glanced over at me. "Yes, it does. Do you think Gunner is right about Larry?"

"I can't imagine why Larry would make up such a self-condemning story. He appeared to be mortified over the whole thing."

"There's no chance he could be an attention seeker and wanted your sympathy?" she asked.

"I can't imagine it. His story put him in a pretty bad light."

"Okay," she said. "Fair enough. I'm just playing devil's advocate. I'm not defending Beverly. She probably was a thief—but a blackmailer threatening to destroy someone's family? That's a whole different ball game. I don't know how she would have reconciled that with her past."

I drew my gaze from the cattle grazing in the field beside us. "Her past? What do you mean by that?"

"She only spoke about it once. It was when we first met, and we'd had a lot to drink. She told me her father had used the equity in their house for a loan to pay his debts. Financially, things got worse instead of better. He couldn't pay the mortgage and the bank foreclosed—forced them out." Danielle paused as the rumble of a passing truck drowned her words.

"The family moved in with her paternal grandparents," she continued. "They were not honest or good people. She called them con artists. I've been thinking about her growing up in an environment like that. It may have prompted a belief in her that the world owed her, and that the best way to prosper was to take what she could from others before they took from her."

I wasn't surprised to learn this about Beverly.

Danielle continued. "As you can imagine, it wasn't a happy place to live. Her father drank and her mother checked out. Beverly was only sixteen when she left home. She struggled to make ends meet as a server for ten years. Then she met a good guy, and she worked with him in home renovations."

"That must have been Andrew Hill. She married him. I told you how that ended," I said, reminding her that Bev's ex accused her of theft.

"Beverly didn't mention that part. I wonder why the ex didn't go to the police?"

"Maybe he did."

Danielle hit a pebble with her shoe, sending the stone skittering ahead of us. "Maybe. Do you think he could have killed Beverly?"

"He didn't even know she was dead or if he did, he's an amazing actor. I got the feeling Beverly was old news to him. He seemed to be doing well. I don't know why he'd suddenly murder her after all these years, even if she stole from him."

"I guess that makes sense. I may know why Beverly stole that money."

"Oh? Why?"

"I think she did it for her niece."

I stopped walking and stared at her. "She had a niece?" Could that be Hannah Wyatt?

"Yes, her sister had a daughter. That was another tragic story. Her sister died from hepatitis. Although now I wonder if Beverly didn't invent a niece to play on my sympathy."

"What do you mean?" I asked. We started walking again.

"I told you Beverly planned to start a home renovation business. She had experience, right? She said she didn't make enough money as a professional mourner to save her niece from her crappy lot in life and believed the renovation business would give her the opportunity to help this young woman go to college."

I felt some sympathy for Beverly and was reminded we often don't know what people had been through, the history that influenced their choices, behaviors, and beliefs.

"Did Beverly—?" I cut myself off. I'd nearly asked her if Beverly's niece was named Hannah Wyatt. I had no way to explain how I knew this name. Maybe there was some truth woven into Beverly's lies—a niece named Hannah that Beverly cared about and wanted to help, even from the grave.

Danielle looked at me, waiting for the rest of my question.

"What was her niece's name?"

"Um..." Danielle thought about it. "I only heard the name once. It was something like Holly. No, that wasn't it. Maybe Hannah."

Bingo. Hannah Wyatt was Beverly's niece.

I wanted to change the subject, so Danielle wouldn't ask why I wanted to know Beverly's niece's name. "You said Beverly was putting together a team for the renovation business she was starting or pretending to start. Getting back to the blackmail threats, did Beverly mention the name of her potential business partner?"

"I don't recall. I was up to my armpits with my own business and trusting to the point of stupidity, not to mention blinded by love."

"As I said before, Beverly was a professional."

Something was niggling at me, and I didn't want to forget to ask. "You said Gunner introduced you to Beverly. Why?"

"Gunner and I hit it off during that marketing seminar. We were both excited about implementing the new strategies. When we learned we lived nearby each other, we decided to meet in person to do the suggested exercises. Meeting with Gunner made me accountable to get those exercises done.

When we met, I liked him immediately. We were good working partners, but then it became apparent Gunner wanted to get more personal. I explained why this would not work between us. One time, we met over dinner, and he brought Beverly along. He said she was interested in learning about our marketing strategies. The chemistry between Beverly and I... Well, I'd never experienced anything so sudden and intense." Danielle lowered her head, watching her shoes.

It was obvious her heart hadn't caught up to the truths she'd learned about Beverly. It was impossible to reason with the heart. It took its own sweet time to recover. I could relate. We'd both been betrayed by someone we loved.

"Sometimes, I hate her so much," she said. "As much as I miss her, I don't want to feel this way anymore, but I can't stop thinking about it."

The whole thing was messy, but I hadn't gotten to this stage in life without gaining a bit of wisdom. "I know it hurts. I've found that if I sit quietly and focus on whatever emotion comes up, believe it or not, those horrible feeling start to diminish. It doesn't happen overnight, but it helps eventually. We're going to have to forgive Beverly and Bryan, not to say their behavior was acceptable, but to free ourselves from their hold. They don't get to destroy us."

Danielle was quiet for a minute. "Okay, thank you. I'll try that. I have to learn to trust again, and that's going to start with trusting myself not to be fooled into making another costly mistake."

I was going to have to work on that, too. Right now, my world was upside down. I wondered if I'd instigated Bryan's betrayal because I'd pursued my dream and gone ahead with the café against his judgment. Had I been selfish like he'd accused? But that wasn't fair. Why would I blame myself for his affair? But...but...but. I was giving myself mental whiplash.

"We mustn't ruminate," Danielle said, as if reading the waterwheel going around in my head. "You have your café opening to think about. You need to focus on that, Quinn. And I have a business to run."

"I know." It was incredibly important to me to succeed.

"Please, for your well-being, don't look any further into your husband's indiscretions. It's not worth it, and it could be dangerous. Someone killed Beverly and we don't know why."

I couldn't argue with that. I didn't need to keep digging into Beverly and Bryan's affair, but knowing what I knew, was I now obligated to help Hannah Wyatt, a young woman I'd never met? Perhaps not obligated, but it was the decent thing to do. Did the keys I'd taken from

Danielle's garden open a locker full of money—Danielle's money? Larry's money? Other betrayed people? Money I could return?

I wanted to tell Danielle about the keys, but there was no explanation for how I knew they were hidden in her yard that didn't come from the mouth of a phantom.

Yes, my café was my priority, but I also knew I couldn't walk away from this. Not yet.

Chapter Twenty-Three

I FIGURED THE BEST way to end this was to finish it—do what Beverly was asking. Even if it happened in the afterlife, ensuring her niece's financial security might be the only decent thing Beverly achieved. Also, in doing so, I might unearth a clue as to who killed her, something the police might not learn otherwise. With Toni's help, I'd have to figure out a way to pass along useful information to the sheriff without disclosing my source.

Bryan said Beverly first came to him to set up a trust, probably for Hannah. This may or may not have been true on Beverly's part if the point of the relationship with Bryan was to blackmail him. If it was true, Bryan might have Hannah's contact information.

Beverly wanted Hannah to receive whatever the seven keys unlocked. I had the keys, but I didn't know what they opened. Something valuable, I assumed. They were small and could be for safety deposit boxes. I wouldn't know until Beverly appeared.

I'd told her to stay out of my life, but I didn't expect her to heed the demand. Now that I wanted to talk to her, I didn't know how to get in touch.

"If you're listening, Beverly," I said to my empty kitchen. Well, empty except for Oreo, who looked up and meowed a response. Conversing with my cat never got old.

I started again. "I have the keys you wanted me to retrieve. I know Hannah is your niece. Maybe you're trying to protect her, but I can't give her the keys if you don't tell me where to find her." I looked from one corner of the room to the other. No ghost.

The doorbell rang, interrupting my fruitless appeal to the otherworld.

I opened the door to see a woman at the end of the driveway swing into a courier truck. She waved from the front window and pulled away. A small white box sat at my feet, about the size of a box of computer paper.

The events of the last few days sent my nerves into a flurry. Was I expecting a package? Not that I could remember. I looked down at the box. It could contain photos I'd never erase from my mind's eye. Photos that could destroy my family and possibly my business.

The box was addressed to me. I picked it up and brought it inside. It was heavier than a box would be if it held a few photos. That was a little reassuring. I tilted it one way, then the other. Inside, something shifted, but only slightly. I didn't recognize the return address, but seeing it eased my trepidation. Surely, a blackmailer wouldn't use one.

Slicing through the tape, I let out the breath I'd been holding and opened the box. Inside was another box, blue with a painted white ribbon. A gift?

Oreo looked at me from the window seat. "What do you think, boy?" He licked his paw.

A possibility popped into my mind. A peace offering from Bryan? An apology gift? Details of a trip to East Asia? I didn't want any of those things.

Stop guessing and open it already.

I wiggled out the gift box, sliced through the tape, and opened the flaps to reveal the new menus for Break Thyme.

Relief melted away the tension in my shoulders. "Well, that's a pleasant surprise," I said to Oreo. How could I have forgotten these? I'd ordered menus for the summer season to fit in acrylic holders, one on each table and three for the counter. I stood back and admired them. They looked great—black, white, and a splash of coral.

The menus were a potent reminder I needed to focus on my café. As I had that thought, a text came in from my designer. Her crew had just delivered the tables and my new, fancy espresso machine. I thanked her.

I called Toni and asked if she'd like to have dinner at Break Thyme. I'd bring a pizza, wine, and the latest update on the swindling spirit saga; the ghost who I now hoped hadn't crossed to the other side, leaving me in the dark.

"No one has been arrested for Beverly's murder," I said to Toni. "You'd think, with the connection I have to the victim, I'd have a solid clue or two, but Beverly has no idea who killed her."

Toni snatched up a crumbled piece of bacon that had fallen off her pizza. "Don't want to mar these tables—they're stunning."

I agreed. I loved the way they'd turned out. The tabletops were high gloss chartreuse with steel legs that matched the counter.

"It's not as if you're trying to solve her murder," Toni said.

"I know, but because I'm so fortunate to be haunted by the dead person, I might know things the police don't."

"That's the spirit. I like the way you always see the sunny side."

"Very funny," I said.

"On the sunny side, there's a niece who stands to inherit the fortune Beverly may have extorted from cheating spouses."

I thought of Danielle. "And innocents. The sunny side has some cloud coverage."

"I guess it does. Do you know if Bryan is still a suspect? The police haven't spoken to you again, have they?"

"No, they haven't." But that wasn't a comforting thought. It could take time for them to build their case. "I would know more about Bryan if he wasn't keeping his distance, which is fine with me. Maybe my statement cleared him, but Beverly's *evidence* is still out there. I don't know if she has something that could save us or hurt us, and I wouldn't be surprised to learn she has nothing at all."

Toni sighed and shook her head. "Bryan didn't give her any money, did he?"

My laugh came out like a snort. "When pigs sprout wings. You know how hard it is to get a dime out of him. I checked our accounts—no suspicious withdrawals." I took a sip of my signature star-anise, blackberry cordial, and soda.

"Beverly must have ripped off other people," Toni said. "The police are probably looking into that. Especially men from that strip club."

"Yes, that makes sense. Actually, it wasn't a strip club. It was some kind of hook-up thing. Like a swinger's club. Anyway, you're right. If I've figured these things out, the sheriff must be two steps ahead of me."

A knock sounded on the front door.

Toni looked over. "Your first customer has arrived!"

I laughed since opening day wasn't for another couple of weeks. "Shift over then. We have pizza and soda on the menu today." I got up and pointed to the sign on the door that said closed.

"I know that," he called through the door. "I have something for you."

I looked at Toni. She shrugged. I opened the door.

The man was heavy, balding, with an unattractive five-o'clock shadow. He handed me a manila envelope. My throat went dry. Was I going to fear packages for the rest of my life?

"What is this?" I asked, unkindly.

"It's an offer to take over the lease," he said.

I looked at him, confused. "I'm not looking for anyone to take over the lease. I'm not even open yet."

"We know that." His smile was patronizing. "Do you know how hard it is to get lakefront, commercial property?"

"No," I said, showing my teeth in a sarcastic smile. "This fell into my lap."

"Well, lucky you. I represent a corporation that has made you an offer you'd be foolish to refuse. Have a look." He gestured to the envelope. "It's all there. They're going to pay you double your rental payment for the next three years to hand over the lease. They want both properties. This one and that extension you've pushed into next door."

"I'm not interested. Not one bit."

He stepped back. "That's not what I heard. I'll give you time to think about it. Like I said—don't be foolish."

"Foolish?" A snappier comeback tripped all over my tongue in outrage as he walked away. All I managed was, "This place must be a goldmine if your client will pay that!"

He kept walking. "Arrogant, son of a..."

Toni was standing behind me when I turned. "What did he mean by that's not what I heard? Who told him you want to get out of your lease?"

I stared at her. That part had gotten lost in my outrage. "Good point. I've never once said such a thing to anyone. Who could—?" I stared at the envelope as the only person popped into my head.

"What?" asked Toni.

"Bryan. It had to be him. He's the only one who wants me out of this café."

"He wouldn't? Would he?"

I could see him doing something like this. Going behind my back. Getting some big corporation to make me an offer I couldn't refuse. That lawyer had been right. Lakefront store leases were nearly impossible to get.

"Can you imagine how the townspeople would react if I signed over this lease to a big box retailer?" The small-town charm of Bookend Bay would be tarnished forever. Sure, we had a few national chain restaurants out by the highway, but in town, locals ran the businesses. Their livelihoods depended on it. If we started selling out to big businesses to make a dollar, it could be the end of Bookend Bay.

I tossed the unopened offer behind the counter. I wanted to throw it in the trash, but I wouldn't do that, not yet. Not until I found out if Bryan was behind this.

Chapter Twenty-Four

I GOT MY WISH the next morning, after breakfast, when I had my head in the freezer. It was the only way to cool down. I'd just experienced a wave of heat radiating from my core to my head. I knew what it meant, but I wasn't ready to say the word menopause out loud.

Behind me, Oreo let go a mewling cry. I bumped my head on the top of the freezer in a panicked attempt to see what was wrong with him.

Standing in the middle of the kitchen, he'd arched his back and was hissing.

Beverly. The phantom finally decided to make an appearance.

I closed the freezer door and rubbed my head. "It's about time."

"I won't ask what you were doing in deep freeze," she said.

"Good." My internal heatwave was subsiding. I hauled Oreo into my arms, whispered soothing words in his ear, and set him on the window seat.

"Let's talk in the living room, so you don't give my cat heart failure." I so needed my life to return to normal.

"This is a dramatic piece," she said, indicating the fireplace that divided the kitchen from the living room. It had been one of the selling features of the house—a stunning expanse of glass-encased flames. I had it going from October to April.

I didn't want to discuss my instant fire. "I have your keys," I said. "And I met another one of your victims. Danielle is a nice person." I stared hard into her pale eyes and realized I could see through her to my Lawren Harris painting of the north shore of Lake Superior. It had been a gift from my mother for our twenty-fifth wedding anniversary. A reminder of what was most important at the moment.

"I want whatever evidence you have, and I want it now."

"Evidence?"

"Don't act coy, Beverly."

Her hand reached for her neck, and I realized her scarf was colorless. I could hardly make out the flowers in her patterned dress. Everything about her was fading away.

She looked around the room. "I used to love stuff like this. You have a good eye for color, Quinn. I like the pops of orange."

I tapped my foot on the floor and gave her my best evil eye. "I'm waiting."

"I see you're one of those people who can't accept a compliment from a friend," she said.

"We're not friends. I don't like you. You've done some horrible things."

"Yes," she said, surprisingly. "That's true. I've been reflecting on my life. It's part of the process here, just so you know when you find yourself...dead. I can see now where it all went wrong. I was a victim myself, you know."

"Maybe, but that doesn't justify the things you did. You've ruined people's lives."

"I've been thinking about that, too. Apparently, it does me no good to deny it. I'm trying to do better, while I still can." She moved to the armchair, reached out as if she intended to touch it, but then pulled her hand back.

"You have the means to fix everything," she said, looking at me. "I was putting everything in place, and I didn't even know it, not until now. Strange how things work. Everything is in motion, Quinn. It's going to be okay."

"What are you talking about? What things?"

"The other side is calling. I don't feel the same attachment to this place. I'm going to leave it all in your capable hands and go."

"Don't you dare leave this—"

She disappeared.

I was staring at the wall, at a painted lake of blue. My phone rang, distracting me from my bewildered thoughts.

I retrieved my phone and saw that it was Danielle. "Hello."

"Quinn, can you come over here right away? I found something. I don't know what it means, but you should see it."

It took me an hour to shower, dress, and get to Danielle's. She opened the door and stood back to let me in. My gaze drew to the other side of the room, to the floor-to-ceiling windows and the view of her garden, which I knew well, and the blue of Lake Superior.

I smelled the remnants of a fire. Strange, considering it was the end of May and a decent temperature outside.

"Come and see," Danielle said. I followed her down a couple of steps into the large room. At one end, there was a magnificent field-stone fireplace, but no fire.

"I found some of Beverly's things," Danielle said. "She didn't have much stuff here, mostly clothes and toiletries. I'd already packed those things to give away. Then I found a couple of boxes downstairs in the furnace room. I didn't know she'd put them there. Honestly, if my niece hadn't asked for the teacups I've been storing forever, I don't know when I would have found Beverly's boxes."

Excitement flowed through me. "What did you find?"

"Don't judge me, okay? I was angry at her. At first, I thought it was just a box of mementos—stuff from high school, so I burned it. It was cathartic, you know, watching her stuff turn to ash."

I gave her a sympathetic smile. "You don't have to explain."

"But then I realized I'd thrown something odd in the fire. Come and look."

On the coffee table sat a cookie sheet holding a few charred pages. She picked up the top sheet. "She never talked about anything like this."

It was a schematic drawing of a rectangular box. Numbers showed a length of thirty-six inches, a width of six inches, and seven inches in depth. I looked at Danielle. "This is an odd size. You don't know what it was for?"

She handed me another drawing that showed boxes fitting into a staircase. Each stair housing one box. "How old are these drawings?" I brushed away a cinder that clung to my sleeve.

"I don't know. I've already checked my stairs if you're thinking she hid the boxes here."

That was exactly what I was thinking. I had seven keys. "Let's have another look."

I followed her to the stairs going up to the second floor. The staircase was contemporary, with geometric balusters, gray-washed wood steps, white risers, and a landing four steps up.

"The only way to access a hidden box would be through the risers," she said. "There's nothing loose. I checked."

I squatted down to have a look. It would have been so handy to find keyholes, but I guessed that would have defeated the purpose of hidden boxes. We checked each stair and found nothing obvious, no splits in the paint seams, no loose boards. We checked the downstairs as well but found no way into the stairs without breaking something.

"I can't imagine Beverly could have had someone come into this house and alter my staircase without me knowing. I don't think there's anything hidden here."

Telling her about the keys was on the tip of my tongue. Maybe I could say Beverly gave the keys to Bryan as part of the trust fund she was setting up, but I didn't have a reason I'd not shared this information earlier. Maybe it didn't matter, but I couldn't think it through quickly enough.

"Where else did Beverly have access to a staircase?" I asked.

"The funeral home," Danielle said, then paused. "There's a staircase to the basement. We stopped there late one night to pick up a pair of shoes she'd left behind."

Yes, she was right. "I don't think we should tell anyone about this until we know for sure."

"That's fine with me," Danielle said. "I don't know if I want to get further involved with this."

I cocked my head toward the sound of the alarm on my phone ringing. "I understand. That's my alarm, and it's a good thing I set it. I need to pick up my son at the airport."

"Okay. You can take the drawings if you like. I have no use for them."

That worked for me. I said goodbye and left Danielle's, feeling like we were both pawns in Beverly's game, and she'd checked out. I couldn't forget someone murdered Beverly and that poking around in her secrets could be dangerous. I just didn't know which secrets were the dangerous ones. Yes, I wanted answers, but I also didn't want to come face-to-face with her murderer.

Chapter Twenty-Five

SINCE I ARRIVED AT the airport early, I decided to surprise my son with a personal welcome, so I parked the truck and entered the terminal. I had a craving for something sweet and saw a concession shop across the small lounge.

"Excuse me," I said as I squeezed by a guy digging through his suitcase in the middle of the aisle. An announcement drowned out whatever he said back to me. Man, it was noisy in here.

It would be nice to be traveling somewhere, escaping the turmoil of my life, even if just for a long weekend like Jordan had done. Again, I thought of the trip Bryan may be planning, but I couldn't imagine us on a holiday together.

I spied the candy display and waited for a woman to step away from the selection of chocolate bars. I knew what I wanted, a Cadbury fruit and nut bar.

"Quinn?"

I turned to see my husband standing behind me. I blinked a couple of times, thrown by his appearance. "Bryan. What are you doing here?"

"Jordan asked me to pick him up. Did he ask you as well?"

"Yes, he did." I sighed. "He wouldn't know we're not communicating with each other." I didn't bother to keep the irritation out of my voice. No point beating around the bush. I stepped away from my chocolate fix.

"Did you send a realtor to Break Thyme with an offer to lease my café?"

"What? No. When did that happen?"

I stared at him for a moment, looking for signs he was lying. It wasn't a habit of mine, so I wasn't sure what to look for.

"You don't believe me," he said.

I was going to remind him he'd not exactly been candid lately, but he didn't give me the chance.

"We need to talk, Quinn. First, I don't want you to give up your café, and I'll tell you why, but not here. Second, I have something to show you."

"What is—?"

"Mom? Dad?" That voice belonged to my daughter, who was five steps away. "What are you guys doing here?"

I looked at Bryan, then back at Samantha. My son couldn't have mistakenly asked all three of us to pick him up from the airport. "Looks like we're all here to drive Jordan and Chelsea home. He's up to something. Let's get over to the arrivals."

We stood near the exit, awkwardly making small talk. At least it felt awkward to me. I don't think Samantha noticed.

"There they are," Samantha said.

Sure enough, my son and his girlfriend were bouncing toward us, backpacks in tow, holding hands and smiling widely.

We all exchanged hugs, then I stood back with questioning eyes.

"I guess you're wondering why I called you all here," Jordan said, smiling at the cliché, I supposed.

"I think we should always do this," said Samantha cheerily. "Next time, we'll have welcome home signs and make it a celebration."

I couldn't help but smile at Samantha.

"I don't think so," Bryan said. He let out his breath. "What's up, Jordan?"

Chelsea gave a little jump. "Can I tell them? We got married in Las Vegas!"

To say I was stunned speechless was an understatement.

Two young women approached, pulling small pieces of luggage. The tall one slowed down and said, "Nice meeting you guys. Congrats again! Long life together!"

"Way to go, bro," said Samantha, hugging her brother. "Congratulations, Chelsea. Is there a ring?"

Chelsea fluttered her finger at us, but everything was a blur to me.

"This is a surprise," Bryan said, sounding more enthusiastic than anything I could muster.

"Mom?" Jordan said, looking sheepishly at me. Then I knew. He asked us all here together to a public place to deflect my reaction. "I hope you're happy for us."

I let out my breath and felt my weak smile. "I—I—all I want is for you to be happy, Jordan. As your dad said, it's a surprise. You and Chelsea haven't been dating very long." Five months was not nearly long enough to know a person.

"I know, but you and dad didn't date long before you got married."

And look how that turned out.

"I was hoping to be at my son's wedding." I forced myself to look at Chelsea, vigorously pushing the thoughts from my head that this was all her doing. I wondered if they'd been drinking before heading for the chapel. "Your mother might feel the same way."

"Actually, she thought getting married in Vegas was a hoot. She wants to talk to you about throwing us a reception party."

My heart felt like a lump of coal. "I see. You've already told your family."

"Yeah," Jordan said. "Chelsea called her mom before the ceremony. I would have done that, too, but I wanted to surprise you guys."

I wasn't sure I believed that. He didn't call because he knew I would have tried to talk sense into his block-of-a-head. Why had Chelsea's mother thought this was a sensible idea? Because she was less pragmatic than me? Did Jordan think she was more of a "hoot" than me?

Bryan leaned close to me. "It's done now," he said in my ear. "Fake a smile, Quinn."

Was my son going to stop confiding in me because he was worried about my practical reactions? "Surprise us, you did," I said, turning my frozen expression into a smile. "I hope you know I truly want the very best for you both."

Jordan beamed. "Thanks, Mom."

"This calls for a toast," Bryan said. "On me."

As we moved our small party to the bar, I tried to smile genuinely. Maybe I'd judged Chelsea more harshly than I should have. Jordan was intelligent and sensible. He saw something in her. Surely, I would be pleasantly surprised as I got to know my new daughter-in-law.

After our toast, Jordan and Chelsea headed home with Samantha, leaving Bryan and I walking to the parking lot on our own.

"Do you think she's pregnant?" Bryan asked.

"Oh, man, I didn't even think of that. I seriously hope not."

"Me too, although we managed okay."

Yes, we had, but it hadn't been easy. When we learned I was pregnant, we did what we thought was the right thing and got married. We'd moved in with my parents so Bryan could finish his business degree. And while our friends traveled, partied, and focused on themselves, we changed diapers.

Lately, I wondered if I would have married Bryan otherwise.

"You said you had something to tell me," I reminded him.

"Yeah. Can you come to my car?" The airport parking lot wasn't vast, so we weren't parked far apart. I followed him to the blue Corolla he'd been driving for the last seven years. He opened the passenger door and reached in to grab something from the seat. Then he handed me an envelope. I couldn't tell by his placid expression if it was good news or bad.

I took the envelope cautiously. "What is this?"

"Open it."

The envelope was addressed to Bryan at his office—PRIVATE. It had been mailed. I looked closer at the postmark and saw a W. Va. stamp. West Virginia? The flap wasn't sealed. I looked in, saw photos, and felt myself stiffen.

I took a breath. The top photo was the photo I'd already seen of Bryan entering the Motor Inn.

I didn't look at him, but shifted to the next photo. It showed a blonde woman and Bryan having a drink together in a lounge at a bistro table. I could tell the woman was Beverly. In the photo, Bryan was smiling. She'd reached out and touched his arm.

"Really, Bryan? You want to share these?"

He stroked his beard like he was grooming himself. "She was flirting, Quinn. I admit this was not a high point in my life. I need you to know the truth. Please keep going."

The next photo showed the two of them heading up a staircase. I didn't understand why he wanted me to see these.

"I went upstairs with her, to her room because she wanted to give me the contact information for the beneficiary of the trust I was setting up."

"Sure, she did. I always meet my bank manager in a motel room."

"I know it was a bad call. Stupid on my part."

"Stupid is one word for it. Faithless, reckless, inconsiderate are a few others. She was playing you. There probably was no trust fund." I didn't believe that and was pleased with myself to have the wherewithal to fish for information.

"Yes, there was," he countered. "That part was true. The trust was for Beverly's niece. She works in a diner in a small town in West Virginia."

Hannah Wyatt. I kept quiet, letting him talk.

"Beverly wanted to give her niece a monthly stipend. There was family mistrust. Bad history. She was worried that if her niece had a lump sum, her grandfather would get his hands on it." Bryan turned his gaze on the photos. "Look, I want you to know the truth of what happened between me and Beverly. The photos show it."

"They were mailed from West Virginia." I checked the postmark again. "The day after Beverly was killed. Are you saying her niece sent them?"

"I don't know, and that's not the point. I don't care where they came from. I did nothing incriminating."

"How long have you had these?"

"They were in my office. I took time off. I just picked them up."

I looked down at the next one. The camera angle was different. Someone took this photo through the window of one of the motel rooms, obviously a setup. Beverly had stood in the perfect position for a clear view.

Bryan put his hand over mine as I saw the next photo. "There's one missing. I have it, but I left it out. It shows a kiss. That's all it was. One kiss. I swear it. Nothing more."

One kiss was enough to make me feel sick. He wanted me to know the truth so he could feel better about this.

The next photo showed Bryan pushing Beverly away. The next one showed his back as he left the room.

"More missing pictures?" I asked.

"No. Nothing further happened. They set me up, Quinn, you can see that, right? Someone was outside taking these photos, just like what happened to that guy, Larry. This is all they have. I did nothing else. They can't blackmail me for this."

"Great. What a relief," I said sarcastically. "Just a kiss in a motel room. You said things got physical. To me, that meant more than a kiss. Why did you let me think that?"

He swallowed. "I'm leaving, Quinn." He'd said it so abruptly, I thought I'd misheard.

"Good. Leave. I have things to do, too."

"No. I mean, I'm leaving Bookend Bay. I'm moving to South Korea. I'm going to do some teaching."

I froze. Everything around me faded to nothing except for the buzzing in my ears. For a second, I thought it was a bee. I shook my head, trying to get my wits back.

South Korea. The pamphlets Mary Carscadden had seen in his room weren't for planning a vacation for the two of us. He didn't want to fix anything. "You won't take a holiday, and now you're moving to the other side of the world? That's it, Bryan? Are you asking for a divorce?"

He shook his head. "No. No, I just—I just need time to figure things out. This thing with Beverly... I left that room because I got spooked. I sensed we were being watched. Otherwise, I don't know that I would have stopped." He said nothing for a minute.

Then I knew what he was saying. Thinking he was being watched stopped him. Not me. Not because he valued our marriage. He didn't want me to break the café lease because it no longer mattered to him if Break Thyme succeeded. He probably hoped it would be an income source for me now.

"I'm sorry for just blurting it out," he said. "I am. I know this is upsetting, but it can't be a surprise. Our marriage has lacked affection for years now."

Unfortunately, he was right, but it had been impossible for me to feel affection when I was under attack all the time. "Maybe if you were less critical and more support-ive."

"We are who we are," he said, unapologetically. "I don't want you to think I had an affair with Beverly—it wasn't that. I don't want the kids to think it."

That's why he'd shown me the photos. So I couldn't tell the kids he'd been having an affair. It was just one little mistake. I wouldn't have told the kids, anyway.

"You know something, Bryan? You want time to figure things out? You can have all the time you need—as a divorced man. You'll be hearing from my lawyer." I tossed the photos on the hood of the car and walked away.

I dreaded telling the kids their parents' marriage was over, but at least they were adults now with their own lives. I was too stunned to think much further than that, although I made a point to remember that Bryan had Hannah Wyatt's contact details if I couldn't get them anywhere else—if I was going to try. The ghostly grifter was only a flicker through my mind.

As I crossed the parking lot to my truck, Bryan didn't call my name. He didn't try to ease the blow he'd just dealt—everything from Beverly to South Korea. He was a class-A jerk, and I was better off without him.

You're going to be okay. Bryan's news would not break me. When the shock of this passed, yes, I was going to be okay. No. I was going to be better than okay. I was going to be better than I could imagine.

Chapter Twenty-Six

INSTEAD OF GOING DIRECTLY home from the airport, I turned down the sideroad that led to the lighthouse. Steadfast and protective, the warning beacon was one of my favorite places in Bookend Bay. On this side of the bay, across from town, the water carved a rocky shore.

From where I sat, I could see the two rock spires bookending the mouth of the river, the ribbon of beach etched into the shore, the boardwalk running through Courtesy Park; the shops bordering the park, and a boat motoring into Moose Harbor.

I breathed in deeply, out slowly, letting my feelings rise and fade away. I had quite a few—sadness, anger, fear, excitement, freedom. And hunger. I checked my watch. It was after 6:00.

By the time I walked back to my truck, I was feeling better, thankful for my support system—my kids, family, friends, community.

I'm leaving Bookend Bay and moving to South Korea.

I moaned into my windshield. I supposed the end of my marriage was going to take more than twenty minutes to recover from.

As I drove back to town, I called Toni. After I told her my news, she was silent for a moment. "I'm sorry, Quinn. I know words are inadequate right now. How are you?"

I took stock. I felt lighter than I had an hour ago. "I'm good—surprisingly."

"I'm glad to hear it and not so surprised. I don't want to beat a dead horse..."

"Oh, please, go ahead, beat away."

"You know I was married to my best friend. I kept nothing from Norman. You deserve a partner you can talk to about anything and everything. Someone who listens, who's engaged. Just like the way you and I share things. I'm not sure when things changed for you and Bryan, but you seemed to filter everything you said because he was in a mood or uninterested."

Leave it to Toni to say it as she saw it although it made me feel like I'd been untrue to myself trying to be someone I wasn't to keep the peace between Bryan and me. I was a strong, capable, intelligent woman about to start a business. I was no mouse.

"Quinn, you must feel lost. This has just been a crazy time for you, but you're going to be okay. You know that, right?" She paused. "Did you eat? Can I buy you dinner?" she asked, possibly taking my silent reflection as a bristle.

"I was just about to ask you to buy me dinner," I joked. "So, yes, please."

Dinner with Toni was the best thing I could have done, and not because of the triple chocolate cheesecake. Well, the cheesecake went a long way to boost my mood.

Toni knew I didn't want her feeling sorry for me, and by the time we got to the cheesecake, I began to see possibilities.

That was saying something. The time it took to consume a bottle of wine, a shrimp scampi, and a chocolate cheesecake had me stepping into a new reality. I knew there'd be difficulties, so I intended to hold on to my good humor as long as I could. Hopefully until bedtime.

"What are you going to do about those keys you got from Danielle's rock garden?" Toni asked after the server cleared our dessert dishes. She knew when I needed a change in subject.

"I'm going to break into the funeral home and tear apart their stairs, obviously."

"Obviously," Toni said and put her napkin on the table. "Before we risk getting caught for that, shouldn't we have a better sense of Hannah Wyatt? What if she's a swindler like her Aunt Beverly was?"

She was right. Taking any kind of risk for someone I'd never met wasn't sensible. "I didn't tell you the photos of Bryan and Beverly were mailed from West Virginia—before Beverly was killed."

"What? From who? Her niece?"

"I don't know. They had other family members there."

"So Beverly was stringing you along," Toni said. "She probably knew the photos would come in the mail but didn't tell you because she wanted you to do her bidding first. Maybe that's why you've not seen her lately."

I drained my mug of decaf. "This kind of loose end will drive me crazy."

Toni waved at the server, requesting the check. "I know. So, for my sanity, we better book flights to West Virginia and see if Hannah Wyatt sent those photos, and why?"

I laughed, but she was right. It was exactly what I wanted to do, but it was also impossible. "How many small towns are in West Virginia? Should we start at the top or the bottom of the state?"

Toni rolled her eyes. "It's Davisville, West Virginia."

"How the heck do you know that?"

"Beverly's ex said so."

"He did? How did you remember that?" My temperature suddenly increased. These internal heatwaves were becoming regular. I removed my sweater and blotted my forehead with my napkin.

"It stood out because Norman's sister's last name is Davis. It made me think I needed to catch up with my sister-in-law."

"That's handy." I opened a map on my phone and looked up Davisville, West Virginia. While Toni paid the bill, I did some quick research, driven by a voice inside my head that was envious of Bryan's new adventure. "If Bryan gets to go all the way to South Korea, we can fly to Charleston." I looked at Toni. "Can you get away?"

Toni put her credit card in her wallet and perked up. She loved an adventure as much as I did. "I'm sure not going to miss out on this. Give me a second, and I'll make a quick call."

While she did that, I looked into flights.

"There's a flight tomorrow," I said when Toni confirmed she could get a couple of days off.

"Let's book it," she said. "Then we'll figure out how we're going to ask Hannah Wyatt if she sent those pictures to your husband."

Chapter Twenty-Seven

WE CAUGHT AN EARLY flight the next morning and rented a car at the airport in Charleston, West Virginia. Davisville was about ninety minutes north of the airport.

As Toni drove, I got a call from my contractor to say they'd installed the flooring in the Nook and it looked great. "Thank you, Ray. I can't wait to see it. I'll be back tomorrow evening."

Things were moving ahead again at Break Thyme after the fallen tree. Dishware and cutlery were waiting to be unpacked, washed, and put away. I'd do that as soon as I got back to Bookend Bay.

Drizzle slid down the car window and cast a misty sheath over the trees. I caught my reflection in the side-view mirror and sighed. My hair was frizzing. Now that I'd be a single woman, I wondered if I'd be more attuned to my appearance, more motivated to lose the extra pounds I'd gained in my forties. To what end? I couldn't imagine dating. The thought was terrifying, so I brought my mind back to the present.

Last night, we'd used Google Maps to get familiar with the town of Davisville. It made Bookend Bay look like a metropolis. Davisville had a gas station, a fire department, a school, a pizza place, and a Grill & Chill where, thanks to Toni's genius, we now knew Hannah Wyatt worked.

Toni had called the restaurant and asked if they'd found her glasses, the ones she thought she'd left behind. She remembered her server being a lovely woman by the name of Hannah. It was no surprise the woman who'd answered the phone couldn't find any glasses, but she said she would check the next day when Hannah worked her shift.

We pulled into the Grill & Chill at 1:35. "Are you ready for lunch?" said Toni, turning off the car.

"I'm ready for the bathroom, that's for sure," I said, opening the door. Outside, the smell of char-broil hung in the air. "I haven't had a hamburger in ages."

Toni yanked up her hood and sniffed. "Smells like you're in luck."

A sudden sheet of rain fell from the sky, so we booted it inside. I pulled down my hood, patted my hair, and swiped droplets from my jacket. Before approaching the host, we hung back to look around. It would be helpful to sit in Hannah's section if we could figure it out. I hoped she resembled her aunt.

It was busier than I would have predicted, considering the small town. Maybe the rain brought people in. There looked to be three servers. One was dark-skinned, so she likely wasn't blue-eyed Beverly's niece, although we couldn't rule her out. The other looked to be middle-aged.

"Look. Over by the window." Toni lifted her chin in that direction.

I waited for the fair, blond woman, hair pulled into a bun, to turn. When she did, my first thought was, she's got her aunt's boobs. These women were buxom.

"Out of the three, I think she's our best bet. Let's go."

We stepped forward and asked for a window seat. They'd set the table for four, so we hung our coats on the backs of the vacant seats. The host handed us menus and said our server would come to take our orders.

I opened my menu, peeked over the top, and turned to see where the buxom woman had gone.

"I think I'll have fish and chips," said Toni. "If it clears, we can walk off calories tonight." We couldn't get a flight back until the next day, so we were going to find a motel.

"Here she comes," I said, under my breath.

The woman smiled as she set down two glasses of water. "Hello, I'm Hannah, and I'll be your server today. Do you need more time with the menus?"

It was her! I glanced at Toni before I asked, "Do you have any specials?"

"Not really, no. The soup is homemade, though. We always have Chicken Noodle and today we've got Curried Squash with Apples."

"That sounds good," said Toni. "We're on a little road trip, having some girlfriend time."

"That must be fun. Are you staying in the area?"

"We are for the night," I said. "We were hoping to do some hiking, but with this weather, I don't know."

"Oh, it's supposed to clear up," Hannah said. "I checked since I promised to take my son to the park after school. I won't hear the end of it if that weathercaster is wrong."

"You have a son?" I said, smiling.

"Sure do. He'll be three years old next week. The light of my life."

"That's such a cute age," Toni said. "Busy, too."

Hannah nodded. "Can I get you started on drinks?"

I ordered a coffee and Toni asked for a green tea.

"She seems genuine and sweet," I said, thinking she didn't appear to have her aunt's calculated charisma, which was a relief.

"She does, yes." Toni looked down at the menu again. "Hmm, maybe I'll go lighter and have the soup and half sandwich."

"Oh sure, make me look bad." Toni had always been svelte, tiny even. Five years older than me, she was through menopause. I didn't remember her complaining about hot flashes. I'd hoped to go through the change with as much ease, but I'd already put on weight and the last few nights, I'd woken up in a fluctuation between hypothermia and the eternal fires of the underworld.

Toni made a clicking sound with her tongue. "There's nothing wrong with eating a hamburger, just stop when you begin to feel full."

"I know that, but it tastes good."

"Well, then, enjoy it." She leaned forward. "So, when do we tell her why we're here? Shall we just wing it?"

Mmm, chicken wings. I wasn't sure why I was craving greasy food. "Yes, I think we should make small talk first.

Let's get her to like us, so hopefully, she won't feel threatened when we change the conversation."

"You don't think she'll turn out to be a professional liar like Beverly?"

"I don't know, but my intuition says no."

Toni closed her menu and set it on top of mine. "Was it Bryan who said the grandfather was a crook?"

I was losing track of who said what. "Somebody said that."

The middle-aged server approached the table with our drinks. After she put them down, she asked if we'd made our meal decisions.

"We're with the other server—Hannah," I said.

This server had a face full of freckles. "She's taking a break—on a long shift today. I'll place your order. Do you know what you want?"

"How long is her break?" I asked, then realized that sounded strange. "Never mind, I'll have a burger and a chef's salad instead of fries." This combination satisfied both my sensible and indulgent inner voice.

Toni ordered the squash soup and a turkey sandwich on whole wheat.

"Well, that's inconvenient," I said when the server walked away.

"Yes, rather. Hopefully, it's not too long."

The other server brought our meals and even though we ate slowly, there was still no sign of Hannah. She cleared our dishes. We were now the only two customers left in the restaurant.

"This is a disaster," I said, feeling my hands starting to sweat. "I'll have to tell somebody we need to speak to Hannah. I'm buying lunch, by the way. Thanks for coming with me."

"Thank you, and you know it's no hardship. I'm going to use the washroom. I'll be right back."

I fidgeted until the server brought the bill. Maybe we'd have to come back for dinner and speak with Hannah then.

"I'm paying with credit," I said. "I need to speak with the other server, Hannah. Do you know when she'll be back?"

The server handed me the debit machine. "I'm sorry. I don't know what Hannah's shift is today."

I plugged in a fifty percent tip and finished the transaction, handing her back the keypad. She tore off my copy and looked at the amount. "Thank you!"

"You're welcome. Can you please find out when Hannah will be back? It's important."

"Sure. Give me a minute."

I looked up to see Toni scooting past the tables toward me. "Come on," she said. "I found her. She's sitting at a table by the bathrooms."

I grabbed my purse and jacket and followed Toni to the back of the restaurant and around a corner. Tucked up against the wall with her back to us, Hannah sat alone in a booth with her head down."

I acted as if I'd just noticed her on the way to the bathroom. "Hi again," I said, infusing my voice with charm. She was working on math problems, looked like geometry. "Oh boy, that stuff used to give me nightmares."

Hannah looked up and saw the direction of my gaze on her notebook. "Yes, many people feel that way about calculus. I actually like it."

"That's great. You can't be doing this just for fun. You must be in school?"

She let out her breath softly. I saw worry behind her eyes. "It's an online course to pick up the math I'll need for a science degree. I'm not sure how I'll pay for vet school." She gave a small laugh. "Especially with a three-year-old, but he's the reason I'm doing this. I want him to grow up believing anything is possible. You've got to have dreams, right?"

"I do believe that, yes." So far, I liked her and was really hopeful I'd be able to help with that on Beverly's behalf. I had to admit at that moment I also liked Beverly a little more for trying to help this young woman. "Sometimes things have a way of working out, Hannah."

"Oh, you found her, Mrs. Delaney." It was the middle-aged server. I startled at the mention of my name, but then realized it was on my credit card.

I looked back at Hannah, who had closed her books and was sliding out of the booth. Toni and I stepped back, but we were still in her way.

"I have to get back to work," Hannah said.

"Can I have a minute of your time first?" I asked.

"No, I can't, sorry."

"You can come back after her shift?" the other server suggested, looking at Hannah.

"Okay. Sure. What time is that?" I asked.

"F-five." Hannah squeezed past us and hurried around the corner. The other server followed, leaving Toni and I standing alone.

I looked at Toni. "Was that strange? The way she ran off."

"Yes. She seemed nervous. Do you think she recognized your name? If she sent the photos to Bryan, then she'd know his name was Delaney."

"Right. It seemed odd she didn't want to hear what I had to say. She didn't even ask what it was about."

"Mmhmm," Toni said in agreement.

We started back toward the exit at the front door. I looked around but didn't see Hannah.

Toni was right. Hannah could have recognized my name, which meant she'd mailed the envelope to Bryan. Anyone associated with Beverly should be treated with caution. We didn't know if Hannah had been working with her aunt.

You've got to have dreams, right?

Darn right. On the other hand, I believed Hannah was a hard-working mom, possibly a single mom, trying to better herself for her son. If I could help her reach her dreams, I was determined to make that happen. We needed to talk to her, but I didn't feel confident she wanted to talk to us.

Toni handed me the keys. "Your turn."

Inside the car, I put the keys in the ignition. "Something is wrong. I don't want to leave. We should watch the restaurant in case she leaves before her shift ends."

"I think you're right." Toni shifted in her seat to look out the back window. "Let's make it look like we're driving away. We can turn around and park across the street, maybe down the side of that building over there. Do you see where I mean?"

I followed her gaze. "Yes, okay. We'll hang out there until Hannah finishes her shift."

Chapter Twenty-Eight

WE HADN'T BEEN PARKED longer than ten minutes when a woman in a yellow rain slicker with the hood up, although it wasn't raining, rushed out of the Grill & Chill.

"Is that her?" Toni said.

"I think so. I should have brought binoculars." Ever since the kids were little, I'd kept a pair of binoculars in the truck. We used to bird watch.

"I remember those navy runners," Toni said. "It's her. She really should get herself a better pair of shoes since she's on her feet all day."

"Maybe she can't afford decent shoes." I turned the ignition and waited while Hannah ran to a beat-up blue sedan.

"I think my mother had that Buick—in 1980." Toni fastened her seatbelt and rubbed her knee.

"Are you okay?"

She let out a sigh. "Yes, I'm fine. Just a little sore. It's the rain. I hope I don't have arthritis."

"I hope not, too." The Buick backed out and exited the lot, turning right onto the old highway. "I've never followed anyone before. Well, not sneaky like this, not anyone who didn't know I was following them." I left our hiding spot and pulled out at what I thought was a safe distance behind Hannah.

"Have you tried an anti-inflammatory for your knee?" I asked.

"I just started taking glucosamine. I'll keep you posted."

Up ahead, Hannah turned left. I slowed down and made the turn, keeping back. It was a narrow, worn road with small houses, well distanced from each other. A couple of minutes later, she turned into a driveway. I pulled over onto the shoulder and stopped the car.

"This is probably her house," Toni said. "What are we going to do now?"

I lay my hands on the top of the steering wheel, waiting for Hannah to get out of the car. "Good question. It seems like we spooked her because she didn't finish her shift, or she lied about when her shift ended. Either way, we're going to find out why."

"What's she doing in her car still? Maybe she's on the phone."

From where we'd parked, we could see Hannah, but we couldn't see what she was doing. Two minutes later, the car door opened. She hurried up the driveway, past a parked car, and up the steps to the front porch of the bungalow.

The door opened, and a little person sauntered out wearing a blue raincoat and boots.

"That must be her son," I said.

Hannah appeared to be speaking to a person inside the house. Then a woman stepped out onto the porch and hugged her, then hugged the little boy.

Toni grabbed my forearm. "We can't sit here. She might drive right past us when she leaves."

"You're right! Duck down in case she looks our way." I lifted my hood, put the car in drive, and continued down the road. Hannah was coming down the driveway but had her attention on her son.

"You can sit up, now," I said to Toni when we were past. I drove slowly, since we didn't know which way Hannah would go. Toni watched out the rear window.

"Shoot, she's coming this way. She's behind us now."

"I see her. I'll try to keep a suitable distance between us." As I said it, I could see her gaining on us, so I stepped on the gas.

Toni faced forward and lowered the visor. "I wonder what Miss Marple would do if she was being followed by the person she was supposed to be following."

"I don't know how we can get behind her, not on this road. It doesn't look like she's going back to work today, not with her son."

"Maybe she got a call that he's sick?"

"Maybe, but I don't think so."

We drove for about five minutes before Hannah pulled into a driveway on her left. "She's stopping," I said, watching her in the rear-view.

"You better keep going," Toni said. "We can turn around when we're out of sight and come back."

"Okay. We'll do that." I turned into a driveway, then backed out to return to the house where Hannah had entered. There was no other car in the driveway, so she was probably alone. I was feeling pretty confident she knew something about those photos mailed to my husband. I was going to get answers.

I pulled into the driveway behind her car.

"Okay, so we're no longer on a covert mission," Toni said.

"Nope. I'm going to knock on her door and be honest—well, not honest about her dead aunt visiting me, but upfront about the rest, so she'll know we're not trying to cause her any trouble."

We got out of the car. This house could probably be designated a shack. It couldn't have more than two small bedrooms. The paint was peeling, but the yard was tidy, and the front door was clean and cobweb-free, even in the corners.

Beside the screen door was a bell. I rang it and we waited. A minute later, I rang it again, listening to hear that it worked. It did.

"She's not answering on purpose," Toni said. "I hope we're not scaring her."

I pulled the screen door open and knocked. "Hannah, please open the door. We're not here to cause any trouble."

Everything was quiet inside.

I knocked again. "I have something to tell you about your Aunt Beverly. It's good news. Please. We just want to talk to you." I hoped my promise of good news was true, that I had something of value to tell her. Something good locked in seven boxes.

I looked at Toni, my short, middle-aged friend, standing there with arthritic knees. "Surely, she doesn't think we're any kind of threat."

I heard a latch turning. The door made a scraping sound as it opened to reveal Hannah, fire in her eyes and a baseball bat gripped in her hands. I looked at the bat. She appeared to be using it for protection and not to attack us. Why did she feel the need to arm herself? Had someone threatened her?

"How did you know my aunt?" she asked.

"We'll stay right here on the porch and talk through the screen door," Toni said.

I let go of the door, so it closed between us. "Your aunt was involved with my husband." No sense beating around the bush.

"I know nothing about that," she said, but didn't look surprised. "I haven't seen Beverly in fifteen years, so whatever she did, I can't help you."

"I can help *you*, though. My husband set up a trust for you from Beverly."

She didn't look surprised by that either, so I figured she'd had some word from her aunt in fifteen years, or maybe from Bryan.

"She really did that?" Hannah said, now looking bewildered. "She had money enough for a trust fund?"

I didn't know if there was money in the trust she'd set up. I feared not or Beverly's ghost wouldn't have asked me to retrieve those keys.

"I think there's money, yes, but I don't know for sure." I shifted on my feet, feeling a kink in my back from sitting so much that day. "Hannah, I believe you mailed an envelope to my husband, Bryan Delaney. It was postmarked from here."

Suspicion flickered in her eyes. "I only did it because Beverly told me to do so if she died suddenly."

"So, you have seen her?" Toni asked.

"No. I haven't."

Behind her, a little boy came down the hall. White-blonde, short hair, and a T-Rex on his shirt.

Hannah quickly flicked the lock on the screen door and turned to her son. "Can you please stay in the kitchen, Lucas? I won't be too long."

"I can't get this open. I want a bar." He was holding a granola bar in one hand, furiously tugging at it with the other.

"Okay. Give it to Mommy. I'll open it for you."

"I want to play ball," he said, eyes on the bat.

She leaned the bat against the wall. "We'll play ball on our adventure."

Adventure? Did she mean the park, or was she planning to go farther?

She tore off the top of the wrapper, pushed up the bar, and handed it back to him. He took a bite and a piece hit the floor.

He looked down. "Oops."

"In the kitchen, monkey," she said, picking up the piece and eating it as he bounded back down the hall.

I thought it impressive Hannah kept her composure with her son considering how worried she seemed to be.

"Hannah, please don't think we're any threat to you," I said. "I'm just trying to clear up a few things and need to know about the envelope you mailed to my husband."

"I didn't look inside. I'm not involved in whatever my aunt was doing."

"But you have a reason to feel threatened," Toni pointed out.

"Well, she *was* murdered." Hannah looked from Toni to me, then let out her breath. "About six weeks ago, I received a package, birthday gifts for my son and a letter for me. From Beverly. She was four months late for Luc's birthday, but she wouldn't know that since she'd never met him. The package also contained a sealed envelope addressed to Bryan Delaney."

She crossed her arms over her chest. "Beverly said there was a power of attorney in the envelope for Mr. Delaney to act on her behalf. She also said she was going to make good on her promise."

"What promise was that?" I asked.

"To help my son and I become financially secure. She wrote to me after my mom died; said her worst regret was that she never helped me and my mom. I didn't write her back because I didn't know if I could trust her. My mom once told me Beverly was fascinated by their con artist grandfather and got sucked into the family's criminal ways. My mother was mortified to have a family like that. When she got pregnant, she didn't want them near her child so, she ran away and never went back."

Hannah glanced down the hall. "They say the apple doesn't fall far from the tree. I'm proof of that, too. Lucas and I are on our own, with no family to fall back on. Like mother, like daughter."

"Does your son not see his father?" I asked.

She scoffed. "Gosh, no. When I told him I was pregnant, that was the last I saw of him. The only good to come of that man was Lucas."

"It sounds to me like you're a wonderful mom, Hannah," Toni said.

She gave a slight smile. "Thank you. There's nothing I won't do to protect him." She rubbed her arms and looked behind her again toward the sweet sounds of her son singing in the kitchen.

"I'm not staying here," she said. "I don't feel safe, not with Beverly's killer still out there, and not now that you found me..."

"Oh, dear," said Toni. "I can't imagine we've put you in any danger."

I had the terrifying thought that maybe Beverly's killer was looking for those keys, too. Was it possible they thought Hannah had them? I didn't know if I should tell the police or if that would incriminate me.

"Is there something we can do to help you, Hannah?" I asked, feeling terrible that we'd scared her. I wished I could tell her she wasn't in danger, but I couldn't be sure that was true. I should have grilled Beverly on the circumstances of her death, but I'd been more focused on me and Bryan than I'd been on her murder. I wished I could start over again.

"No. I'm okay," Hannah said. "I've got money saved for my first two years of school, so I'll use that. When the police catch Beverly's killer, I'll feel better."

So, now she was going to have to use her education fund to keep safe.

She put her hand on the inside door, getting ready to close it.

"Hannah, there is a trust fund," I said. "You need to keep your contact information up to date with my husband. Actually, not with him personally, but with the bank," I added, remembering Bryan was leaving the country. "Do you have the bank's contact information?"

"Yes, I do. I'll keep in touch with the bank."

"Good," I said. "Thank you for talking to us. Be safe, Hannah. Please don't give up on your dream. You're going to get through vet school. I do believe that."

"Yeah, sure. Goodbye." She closed the door. Toni and I walked back to our rental car.

When we were inside, I turned to Toni. "I feel just awful for her. I can't imagine being a single mom trying to survive on a server's salary. I'm amazed she's saved any money at all."

"Me, too," said Toni. "We have to do what we can to help her, Quinn."

"I agree. I got the impression Beverly was killed before she could deposit money in the trust for Hannah. I don't think a power of attorney works once you're dead, but I don't know for sure."

Toni took a couple of mints from her pocket and hand-ed me one. "So, if we find money, can Bryan deposit it into the trust fund Beverly set up for Hannah?"

I unwrapped the mint. "I have no idea, but I think an executor could do it. Now, all we have to do is find whatever is unlocked by seven keys."

Chapter Twenty-Nine

THE NEXT AFTERNOON, WE arrived back in Bookend Bay. Since we'd left Toni's car at the airport, she dropped me off at home. I planned to spend the rest of the day at Break Thyme unpacking and washing dishes and glassware.

I unlocked the back door that led into the kitchen. Inside, I found plates stacked on the counter beside glasses and mugs sitting on tea towels. My bottle of bleach sat beside the faucet. It looked like someone had washed all the dishware.

Who did this? I was baffled. No one had a key except for my contractor. Had Ray let in one of my kids or my new barista? I couldn't imagine someone doing this without my asking. Especially my kids, come to think of it. It had often been a struggle to get them to put their dishes in the dishwasher.

I set aside that mystery and checked on the flooring in the Cozy Nook. It looked beautiful! The smoky-gray vinyl resembled hardwood planks and brightened the room, despite the plywood over the windows.

As I put the dishes away, I thought about the decision Toni and I made to do some investigating at the funeral home, the stairs in particular. We'd try to find whatever Beverly meant to go to her niece.

I left the café and went home for dinner. Lately, every time I entered the house, I wondered if Bryan would show up to pack his things or if I'd find an empty closet.

At this point, my attitude was good riddance. As each day passed, I saw things more clearly, especially my marriage. He'd been holding me back. He'd had me second-guessing myself for years.

Maybe my café wouldn't survive, but if I went through life risking nothing, then I was guaranteed to have gained nothing. I would not let the fear of making a mistake stop me from following my dream. I couldn't live like that. Bryan would never support this reasoning. He'd made that clear.

Ending our marriage was the right thing, but it didn't stop my heart from hurting. I felt better when I kept busy.

I checked my watch and saw it was time to pick up Toni. The funeral home closed at nine, and we had to be there before the doors were locked. We planned to check the staircase right away. Hopefully, we'd be able to tell if there was a fake panel hiding boxes. If so, we'd find some place to hide until everyone had left the home.

Toni made me laugh when I saw she'd dressed all in black. She looked like a jewel thief, which was appropriate, I admitted, for our funeral home hunt.

We drove to Nodsworth Funeral Home, but instead of parking in their lot, I parked down the road at a gas station. I didn't want any of the staff questioning whose car was still in the lot after closing hours.

I felt my phone vibrate in my pocket, signalling a text had arrived. "Did you silence your phone, Toni?"

"Good point. I'll do that now."

I retrieved my phone and read the text. "I have a strange message from Danielle. Must be a typo." I showed it to Toni.

She read the text. "*I was the eating? Going to my mom's.* What does that mean?"

"Her phone must have auto-corrected."

"Those messages make me laugh," Toni said.

"I know. I hope nothing serious happened to her mother. I worry about getting a call like that. My mom's so far away I'd have to take a plane to get to her."

"I hope Danielle's mom is okay," Toni said and fished her phone from her pocket. "Okay, my phone is silenced."

I asked Danielle to clarify her message and told her I'd turned off my phone and would check back in a couple of hours.

I retrieved a handbag I'd filled with a few tools we might need. We left the truck and walked up the street to the funeral home. There were still quite a few cars in the parking lot.

"I hope Joyce isn't working tonight," I said as we walked up the stairs. "She's the woman I talked to last time—the one who told me about Larry. I don't know how I'll explain myself if we run into her."

As we opened the door, a man on his way out nodded and waited for us to enter.

"It's busy tonight," said Toni. "There must be a visitation or two if we're lucky. It's less likely we'll be noticed."

We were both familiar with the funeral home, having paid respects over the years. Straight ahead was a hallway with visiting rooms on either side and a small chapel at the end. We passed a glass case displaying a selection of urns. I adjusted the bag of tools on my shoulder and cringed when they clinked.

Toni's eyes darted to me. I glanced inside one of the viewing rooms. An open casket sat off to the side. A few people quietly milled about, but no one looked our way. And really, why would anyone care about a clink? My senses were heightened, and I was self-conscious. I reminded myself there was no reason for anyone to look at us twice.

The kitchen, sitting room, and bathrooms were on the lower level, accessed by the staircase at the end of the hall. We stood at the top of the stairs, looking down. Four stairs, then a landing, then the staircase turned to the left. Each stair had a gray-and-white-patterned carpeted tread leaving the risers exposed.

"This would be where Beverly hid those boxes if they're here," I said quietly and stepped down to the landing. I crouched over the fourth step and examined it. I saw nothing that could be removed. No break in the cream-colored paint between riser and stringer. I would have checked the other three, but the pounding of little feet running toward us stopped me. A curly-haired boy looked down at me. I smiled and said hi. He ran back the way he'd come.

"I don't see any gaps," I whispered to Toni as we reached the basement level.

I'd silently counted the second set of stairs—seven. My pulse picked up. Seven keys for seven stairs?

Overhead, it sounded like people were leaving the funeral home. Downstairs, where we were, a long hall ended at an exit door. There was no one in sight. All was quiet down here.

We both bent over to examine one riser, Toni on the left, me on the right. It wasn't until I got closer; I saw a difference between these risers and the ones above. These risers were not painted into the tread or the stringer. There were razor-thin gaps on all four sides.

"Look!" I said to Toni, pointing to the gaps.

"I see it," she said. "It looks like a panel. Do you think it can be removed?"

"There's a good chance. Yes."

"Okay, so we hide until everyone leaves."

I nodded. "Hopefully there's a closet down here." The first doors in the hallway were for washrooms. "We can't hide in the washroom. They likely get cleaned at the end of the day."

Next, on the right side, was the kitchen.

"I don't see a closet," Toni said under her breath as we entered.

The hushed sound of a conversation made me freeze. Two people sat at a table talking softly and drinking a refreshment. A third woman stood leaning over their table. "It's nearly nine o'clock," she said. "I'm going to go. We'll see you tomorrow morning."

"Okay. Thank you, Sadie," said the man who was still sitting across from a dark-haired woman.

"I could use a coffee before we go," I said as the visitor left the kitchen. I didn't want one. The caffeine would keep me up half the night, but we needed a reason to stay downstairs.

"Okay," Toni said. "Take your time. I'll be in the bathroom." Considering neither of us could go far without a pee break, it was a good idea to stop there first.

I poured a coffee. Since the two people were deep in conversation and didn't look like they were leaving anytime soon, I left the kitchen and met Toni in the washroom.

"Let's check out those doors down the hall," I said quietly, when we were done.

We crept to the first door. A crematorium according to the plate on the door.

"It's warm," said Toni, her fingers touching the wood. "Let's not hide in there. We might get fried."

"Right. Not a good look for us." I moved to the next door and turned the handle, but it was locked.

"Looks like the casket showroom," Toni whispered from across the hall, peering inside a window in the door. She turned the handle, and it opened.

"Caskets it is," I said. We went inside and closed the door. The waning sun from the basement windows cast the room in dim light. Half a dozen different styles of caskets sat on stands. Two large metal people-sized boxes were tucked up on a shelf against the wall.

Toni ran her hands along a wicker casket. "We had one of these for Norman."

"I remember." At the time, I'd never seen a woven casket, but I'd learned they were eco-friendly and biodegradable.

"His was made from seagrass."

"Oh? I didn't know that."

Toni smiled softly. "It was handmade, mostly from willow, but there was seagrass woven into it. I'd liked that idea since he loved the water so much."

"He would have appreciated that, Toni. Besides, Norman was an avid recycler."

Toni laughed. "Remember, he wouldn't put any food in plastic?"

I smiled. "I remember. He got me onto glass. I rarely use plastic these days."

"Me, too. I like the bamboo produce bags I bought from The Horn of Plenty."

I touched the cool surface of a metal casket. "I love that store. When I think of Norman, the first thing that comes to mind was when he told Samantha to be sure to wash her face every morning because her pillow probably carried more bacteria than a toilet seat."

Toni gave a soft snort. "The look on Samantha's face was priceless, especially after the education in how dust mites love to feast on skin cells."

"Before that, I didn't think she knew where the washing machine was," I said. "I never saw a teenager get her pillows into hot water so fast."

We heard footsteps outside the door and what sounded like a cleaning cart rolling by. We both ducked. Across the hall, a door opened.

"Do you think they'll come in here?" I whispered.

Toni stood and ran her finger along the top of the ornate wood. "There's no dust."

I tiptoed over to the door and peeked out the window. Sure enough, a cleaning cart sat in the hallway just outside our door. I scooted back to Toni. "The cleaner is right here," I whispered. "Where are we going to hide?"

She patted the casket. "Inside?"

"Are you out of your mind? We're not climbing inside a casket. We'll have nightmares for life."

"Aren't you just a little curious?"

I finally found one thing that did not pique my curiosity. "Not in the least."

"There's nowhere else to hide in here." She took a few steps toward the metal casket on the low shelf. "It's not tight against the wall. One of us can crawl in behind."

I saw what she meant. "Can't we both fit back there?"

"If we were twelve." Toni sat her bum on the platform that held the ornate wooden box. The top was half-open, revealing a quilted, satiny lining. "We have to hide now."

Toni was usually the rational, rule-following one. I couldn't believe it when she climbed inside the coffin and lay down with her hands crossed over her chest. "It's pretty comfortable and roomy."

A rattle came from the room across the hall, like the cart was on the move.

"Hurry!" Toni whispered.

I set my coffee on the shelf behind me.

"You're braver than me," I said.

"Put your bag here beside me." She looked small in that box.

As quietly as possible, I slipped it from my shoulder and set it down.

"Close the lid," she said. "Don't latch it!"

"Don't worry. I won't." I closed the casket. Then I crawled in behind the metal container. There was only about a foot of space between it and the wall, so I had to turn sideways. Nose pressed against a human burial vessel, this was a place I never expected to be. I couldn't imagine what Toni was thinking.

Seconds later, I heard the door open and feet shuffling over the floor—lots of shuffling, like back and forth. What the heck was that cleaner doing? The ceiling light popped on. I looked down the length of my body to be sure my legs weren't sticking out beyond the end of the casket. That would be a freaky thing to see.

My heart started to pound as the cleaning person came closer. My breath fogged up the smooth metal in front of my nose. I caught the sound of faint Latin music. The cleaner must be wearing headphones and was dancing to the music.

My nose got a tickle. *Unbelievable.* I carefully slid my hand up and squeezed my nostrils shut. It would be such a cliche to sneeze, but no one had dusted back here in ages, it seemed.

An image popped into my head of the dancing casket cleaner, opening the lid and finding Toni in there. I suppressed a giggle.

A couple of minutes later, the light turned off, the door closed, and the cleaning cart rattled away.

By that time, my arm was going numb. It wasn't easy shuffling back out of there, but I did it. Toni was already sitting up.

"You were right," she said. "That was creepy, but now I know what it was like for Norman."

Toni handed me my bag and boosted herself up onto the edge of the coffin. I grabbed her arm to steady her, so she didn't fall.

"It wouldn't have been creepy for Norman—since he was dead," I pointed out.

"We don't know that, especially now that you've met a ghost. How do we know Norman didn't lie in that coffin, confused, wondering if he was dead?"

"Don't you think your spirit leaves your body as soon as you're dead? What's the point of hanging around?"

"I have no idea. Ask Beverly the next time you see her." Toni was still sitting on the edge of the casket. "It was easier getting up here, than down."

"Here, use my shoulder." She shifted position and made it to the floor without breaking a leg.

"My coffee's gone." I crossed the room to the door and opened it just enough to see the cart was now in front of the kitchen and bathrooms. I closed the door. We were going to be in here a while longer.

Chapter Thirty

As we waited amongst the coffins, a muscle in my leg started to twitch. The reminder of my future resting place was contributing to my restlessness. I wanted to get this over with.

It was nearly an hour before the cleaning cart was locked away. We waited another ten minutes, then tiptoed upstairs to be sure we were alone.

Back at the bottom of the stairs, I set my bag on the floor and turned on the lights. Toni climbed the steps and sat down on the landing. "Shall we start at the top? How are we going to pry this panel of wood off the riser?"

"It must have been made to be removed, right? Or it wouldn't be of much use." I'd brought a pry bar and a hammer. Years ago, Brian and I removed the wood paneling from our basement. I hoped the same process would work here. I didn't want to damage anything.

It helped that the claw end of the pry bar fit perfectly into the gap between the riser and the bottom of the next step. It was a tight fit, but by tapping the opposite end of the bar, I could loosen the panel. It came away with a ripping sound.

"It's held in place with Velcro," I said, seeing the tape. "This is definitely meant to be removed."

"Let me help," said Toni. She pulled as I pried, and the panel came off.

We gave a little cheer. I set the panel on the landing.

"Look!" Toni said. "A keyhole. You were right."

My pulse increased as I retrieved the set of keys. I'd not noticed before, but now I saw the number six on a key. "They're numbered. That's handy." This was number one or number seven, I supposed. I found number one, slid it into the lock, and turned. A click sounded and the stair or the box within the stair popped out about an inch. Enough to hook my fingers in the top to pull it open.

"Caesar's ghost! Will you look at that," Toni said as the drawer came open. "I've never seen so many tidy stacks of money."

"Me neither. Just in the movies. This looks like a lot of money, and there are seven keys!"

"There's no question this money belonged to Beverly, right?" Toni said. "We're not stealing it from a living, breathing person?"

"No question in my mind. She had drawings of these boxes as if she'd had them made. She told me where to find the keys, and she was setting up a trust for her niece. We'll be giving the money to Bryan to deposit on Beverly's behalf, so we're not stealing."

"Quinn, why would anyone keep this much cash hidden away like this?"

I shifted position to sit on a stair below. "I think we know why. The people Beverly blackmailed paid in cash."

"What about those people? Shouldn't we pay them back?"

"Yes, we should, but then we only know about Danielle and Larry, so we could pay them back, but should we try to find the other people Beverly scammed?"

She gave me a look. "Sure. You can forget about Break Thyme, and I'll quit my job, so we have time to find and reimburse the married men who slept with Beverly."

"Okay, good point. Not that. Should we hand it over to the police, then?"

"I don't know. Hannah may not see a dime if we do that."

There was another issue in confessing our part in this to the authorities. "If we tell the police, I have to admit a ghost told me to dig up Danielle's garden, and we broke into this funeral home."

"We didn't break in," Toni said.

"I think that's a technicality. Do you think they'll believe we were testing out the coffins, got left inside by mistake, and just happened upon these hidden boxes?"

Toni shook her head. "So, no police. In that case, how are we carrying this money out of here?"

I'd brought in a couple of grocery bags, but those wouldn't be enough. The rest were in the truck. I rifled through my satchel and handed her a cloth bag with the Horn of Plenty logo. "There's more in the truck. I'll go get it and park around the back."

Forty-five minutes later, we had six drawers emptied, and the contents loaded into the back of my truck. Toni's knee was bugging her, so I turned the key to open the last drawer.

"There's no money in this one." I removed a stack of envelopes. Names, in block letters, were penciled across the fronts. My nerves went tight, imagining what was inside these envelopes—photos to blackmail Beverly's targets.

There were eight, and they were unsealed. I quickly leafed through them, but none were marked with Bryan's name. One said Larry Lewis. I thought of Larry, sucking on his soda at the Black Cap. I didn't want to see what was inside his envelope. The last one had the initials G.O. written on it.

"Are we keeping these?" Toni asked, indicating the envelopes.

"Yes. If they're what I think they are, we'll burn them." Was that good enough? Should we try to do more to catch the blackmailer or leave it in the hands of the victims to go to the police? I was leaning toward the latter. I wanted my life back.

I slid the last drawer into the step. Together, we tapped the false front back in place and looked everything over. The stairs looked perfectly normal.

"No one will ever know we were here." Toni brushed her hands on her pants.

I picked up the envelopes and dropped them into an extra grocery bag. "I wonder if Danielle left an update on her mother?"

"I'm more concerned with getting out of here," Toni said. "I've had enough of this place. I have to use the bathroom again. I'll meet you upstairs."

"Okay. Hurry." Goosebumps rose on my skin. I'd had enough of this place, too.

I went upstairs, down the hall, and waited beside the table with brochures. With the last grocery bag at my feet, I opened my phone and saw another message from Danielle and a missed call.

The message said: *Typo: not the eating.*

No kidding. I read the next message.

Threatened. My house was ransacked.

I stared at the message as its meaning registered. Someone threatened Danielle. Because of the keys I'd taken? *Who? Why?* I typed back.

She was typing a response when a motion caught my attention.

I looked through the window beside the door and saw a figure. It was the funeral director. His gaze was on mine, and it wasn't a happy one. Go figure. There was no good reason for me to be standing in the hallway, especially with a grocery bag full of blackmail photos, if that's what they were. Thankfully, all the money was in my truck.

Toni was still downstairs. I had to warn her, so she didn't get caught. There was an exit downstairs. We'd not used it since it was an emergency exit and might be alarmed. Alarm be damned, we could make a run for it. Maybe he hadn't recognized me.

I shoved the phone in my pocket, grabbed the grocery bag, and bolted. Well, bolted was how it looked in my mind. I didn't get more than three steps before his voice boomed down the hall.

"Stop right there!"

I froze at the command because I'd caught a glimpse of Toni coming up the stairs.

Gunner. His name was Gunner.

At the sound of Gunner's voice, Toni whipped back, out of sight. I willed her to escape out the back door, but feared she wouldn't abandon me. I scrambled for a way to talk the funeral director out of calling the police on us.

"I remember you," he said when I turned to face him. I could see the wheels turning in his head. "What are doing in here?"

He remembered me, so he'd likely recall I'd been asking about Beverly.

Inside my pocket, my phone dinged, indicating another text.

I stayed where I was, about ten feet away from him, and gave a weak smile. "I'm terribly sorry. I know I'm not supposed to be in here, but I do have a good reason for it. I didn't break in, if that's what you're thinking. I stayed after the funeral home closed for the night." I rambled when I was nervous and felt myself sounding like a middle-aged dingbat, which wasn't such a bad idea. "I hid, so the cleaners didn't see me."

"Why would you do that?" he asked.

Chapter Thirty-One

GUNNER'S EXPRESSION WAS WARY, of course. He should suspect a stranger who'd hid amongst his coffins.

A hefty dose of adrenaline coursed through my veins. I forced a slow exhale, so I wouldn't start to hyper-ventilate. I was a terrible liar and nervous that I couldn't pull off a lie, especially on the fly. I'd better keep to the truth as much as possible and hope he sympathized.

"Because Beverly Foster was having an affair with my husband," I said, squeezing my eyes in a pained expression. "I believed she'd left incriminating photos behind when she died—here in the funeral home."

His gaze dropped to the bag I was holding. He took a step forward. "Why would you think she'd left photos here?"

"My husband told me." I sniffled and pulled a tissue from my pocket to dab my nose. "Please forgive my inappropriate behavior."

"You mean criminal behavior," he said, but not unkindly.

He was right. "I've not been thinking clearly since my marriage ended. It's been a nightmare. My husband admitted Beverly was blackmailing him with photos—disgusting ones." My voice cracked perfectly on the last two words. I was pulling this off.

He blinked rapidly, then narrowed his eyes. "Your husband and Beverly took photos of themselves?"

I looked down and nodded. It was close enough to the truth.

"I understand how troubling that would be," he said sympathetically. "There's no sin greater than broken loyalty."

"Yes. Exactly. I haven't slept. I'm...I'm not myself. I've been so worried. I couldn't let my children see such things."

His gaze dropped to the grocery bag again. "Did you find incriminating photos? Here?"

Since I hadn't looked in the envelopes, I could only guess. "I just want to destroy them. That's all. I promise. They have nothing to do with the funeral home."

"Can I see them, please?"

I couldn't think of a sensible reason to refuse, so I handed him the bag. "Photos like this ruin people's lives. I hope you understand I needed to find them."

He looked inside, removed the envelopes, and dropped the bag. It landed on his shoe, but he didn't move. He looked at the names and when he got to the last envelope, his eyes flared. From that one, he took out a sheaf of papers. I saw what looked like spreadsheets.

He went still as the dead. I remembered that envelope was the one with initials on it. I could see them in my mind's eye—G.O. Go. Easy to remember. And then a wave of dread filled me. Could G stand for Gunner? I looked at the brochures on the table beside me to see one with a photo of him. Underneath was a sentence, but I only saw the name. Gunner Olsen. G.O.

"You've looked through these envelopes?" he asked.

I whipped my gaze from the brochure. "Me? No. I was going to look when I got home. I was just on my way out of here."

Gunner flexed his hands. It reminded me of those long fingers and the tattoo—loyalty or death. Wheels started spinning in my head as I remembered what Danielle had said about Gunner getting uptight because she stopped their marketing meetings after she started dating Beverly. He'd complained about Danielle's lack of loyalty.

He'd said the tattoo referred to his loyalty to God, but what if that wasn't true? What if Beverly did something to breach her loyalty to him? She had a partner in her blackmailing schemes. Could that partner have been Gunner? My thoughts were racing. My truck was full of money. Was Beverly stealing from him? If he knew about the cache in the stairs, would he check to see if the money was still intact?

"You're going to show me where you found these envelopes." His tone was harsher now.

"You're making me uncomfortable," I said. "Go ahead. Call the police, or I'm leaving."

He stepped forward and gripped my forearm.

"Let go of me!" I tried to shake off his grasp, but his long fingers were made of steel.

"The photos were behind the coffins." As soon as I said it, I realized my mistake. I'd said photos.

"You did look inside the envelopes."

"Just a glance to confirm they had photos in them. Just Larry Lewis's envelope. I didn't want to see more." I didn't think he cared about photos unless they were of him. He cared what was in the envelope labeled G.O. and that I might have seen it.

He let go of my arm. "I'm sorry." His tone softened. "I'll call the police if you prefer. I'd just like you to show me where you found these."

My heart rate slowed down. Maybe I'd jumped to conclusions. He had every right to be suspicious of me, and I'd rather not have to explain myself to the police.

I hoped Toni had escaped through the emergency exit. Maybe it wasn't alarmed, or maybe she was still hiding on the stairs. The little voice inside my head said don't go into the basement with this man. But I couldn't let him go down there and find Toni. On the other hand, if I led him into the coffin room, Toni could escape and call the police if needed.

My chin was trembling, my hands sweating. "Okay, let's go downstairs. I'll show you where I found them." My voice was shaky for real now. I'd spoken loudly, warning Toni we were coming.

There was no sign of her at the bottom of the stairs. He let me lead the way. When we reached the casket room, I opened the door and stood aside, but he was crowding me, so I stepped into the room.

"See that metal casket there on the shelf. The envelopes were behind it. I hid back there—that's how I found them."

"These envelopes were just sitting there on the shelf? In plain view?"

"I wouldn't say they were in plain view."

"It's after midnight," he said. "You must have found your hiding spot quite comfortable to have stayed so long. What are you not telling me?"

"No. It takes your cleaning staff forever—"

He moved swiftly, pushing me further into the room. By the time I got my footing, the door slammed shut, and I heard a lock turn. Regaining my balance, I leaped to the door. The handle didn't turn. I shook the door violently and screamed at him to let me out.

Through the window, I saw him open the door to the crematorium, then I heard a machine turn on. Had he turned on the oven? I felt a scream lodge in my throat. "What are you doing? People know I came here!" I banged on the window with my fist, doing nothing but hurting myself.

I spun around, searching for anything to use as a weapon. Nothing smaller than a casket.

I had my phone! My hands shook as I reached into my pocket. Empty. Then the other pocket. Empty.

Stunned, I scrambled to remember what I'd done with my phone. I was reading Danielle's text. Gunner was at the door. I put the phone in my pocket.

But it was gone.

Gunner took my phone, and I hadn't even noticed?

Whether or not Toni had escaped, she knew I was still inside. She'd be feeling as desperate as I was right now. She'd call the police.

Think!

Maybe I could push one of the coffins against the door. Barricade myself in until help arrived. The nearest coffin was on a platform, six feet from the door. If I got the coffin onto the floor, it could act as a wedge between the door and platform, so the door couldn't open. As long as the platform didn't slide away.

I'd have to move fast. When the coffin hit the floor, it would be loud, and Gunner would probably come running.

I moved to the head of the coffin and shoved with all my strength. It slid forward. Good! Okay, I could get the coffin onto the floor. I pushed the platform, hoping it was too heavy to move. It didn't budge.

I took a deep breath. Wiped the sweat from my hands. I pushed the coffin again. It slid along the platform, but not nearly far enough to fall off.

I pushed. And again.

The muscles in my arms strained. One more push. The coffin went down with a crash! It was too far from the door to block it. I scrambled around the platform. Pain shot through my back as I got down low to push the coffin forward.

I was almost there when the door opened.

Oh, my gosh. It wasn't tight enough. He could squeeze through.

I wasn't going down without a fight. Adrenaline raced to my muscles as I wobbled to a standing position and braced.

Toni's head appeared in the doorway. She looked at me, then at the crashed coffin. "Hurry! Let's get out of here!"

I didn't know I could vault a coffin.

"Where's Gunner?" As soon as I asked, I saw him lying on the floor, face down, about twenty feet away at the end of the hall by the kitchen.

"I hit him with an urn. You were making so much noise he didn't hear me come up behind him."

"You saved me! Thank you." I gave her a tight hug. "He's not dead, is he?" I asked, letting her go.

"I didn't look, but I can't imagine... Come on. Let's get out of here. I called the police. They'll be here any minute."

The drone of the crematorium furnace sent a chill down my spine.

I hesitated. My mind was racing. "He can say we broke into the funeral home, destroyed a coffin, and assaulted him."

Toni's eyes filled with alarm.

"We have to get the envelope with his initials on it. There's something incriminating in there to make him want to turn me to ashes. Toni, he might come after us to keep us quiet."

"Wh-where is it?"

I didn't know. "He had it with him when we came downstairs."

The exit door was behind us, so we could get out that way—alarm be damned. I swallowed. "I'm going to look for it. You get out of here and lock yourself in the truck until the police arrive." I reached into my pocket for the keys.

"You nearly got yourself fricasseed the last time I left you alone. I'm not—"

"Okay. Okay. Come on. Hurry." I ran down the hall toward the prone funeral director. A shard of the broken urn crunched under my shoe as I darted around him.

Blood. I looked away, my heart pounding.

"Check the kitchen," Toni said, but I could already see the envelope on the counter in front of the coffee maker.

"I see it!" I ran inside, snatched the envelope, turned.

A groan came from the man on the floor.

"He's waking up!" cried Toni.

His arm moved, reaching for his head.

"Run!" I screamed as I flew past him.

I raced behind Toni to the end of the hall. We burst through the exit and ran to my truck. I fumbled with the keys. Hit the lock by mistake.

A screech got jammed inside my throat. The seconds dragged out. I hit the unlock button and heard the blessed sound of the doors unlocking.

We scrambled inside. Locked the doors.

I shoved the key into the ignition and hit the gas before putting the car in drive. The engine roared, and the truck shuddered. I cursed.

"Quinn! Calm down. We're okay."

I looked at Toni, took a breath, then tried again. Success! I reversed out of the parking spot. Sped around the building toward the driveway.

A police car made a hard left, blocking my exit.

"Watch out!" Toni cried.

I hit the brakes.

Chapter Thirty-Two

THEY QUESTIONED TONI AND I at the sheriff's office for a couple of hours. Sheriff Jansen was not happy with our funeral home takeover and made me feel about two inches tall after I told him the same story I'd told Gunner. I didn't mention the money. Maybe that was criminal, but I couldn't think of a reasonable explanation for how I'd known about the keys if Beverly hadn't told me.

The sheriff said the contents of the G.O. envelope we'd retrieved were damaging enough to not only investigate and detain Gunner for extortion, but I also got the impression Gunner was a suspect in Beverly's murder. Sheriff Jansen said that with the evidence I'd left behind at the funeral home, Toni and I didn't need to worry about Gunner getting out of jail anytime soon.

I was relieved when one of the deputies returned my phone. Shortly after, Toni and I were let go with a warning not to hide in any more coffins. We were happy to comply.

Before I took Toni home, we stopped at my house and transferred the bags of money into my furnace room. We'd figure out what to do with the loot after a night's sleep. We were both exhausted and wanted to get to bed.

Surprisingly, I slept through the night and half the next morning without waking. I felt refreshed and remarkably at ease, although I wasn't finished with Beverly's mess yet.

Once I'd had a coffee, I called Danielle to ask what had happened to her.

"Someone ransacked my house," she said. "Two days ago, Gunner called me and asked what I'd done with Beverly's belongings. He said he was asking on behalf of her family."

"What family?" I said. "He was likely looking for evidence against him. Beverly had something to not only prove he was blackmailing people but might also implicate him in her murder."

"Good grief! What did she have?"

I wished I'd looked inside the envelope with Gunner's initials. "I don't know. I guess we'll have to wait for the sheriff to disclose that information."

Danielle sighed heavily. I told her about the stash of cash Toni and I found in the stairs. "I can reimburse the money Beverly stole from you."

"My money isn't part of what you found. My lawyer is confident I'll get it back from the bank. It's still in her account from what I understand."

"If you're sure about that. I'll be giving the money to Beverly's niece."

"Good. Beverly would have wanted that."

Yes, that much was true. Danielle and I finished our conversation. She said she'd see me at Break Thyme on opening day.

The following week, I ran into Sheriff Jansen at Henrietta's Bakery. He said Gunner confessed to killing Beverly. In Gunner's warped head, she'd been unforgivably disloyal by stealing a target he'd been working on. I imagined this target was Danielle.

"You're not to go digging into any other criminal activity, Ms. Delaney, but I will thank you and Ms. Miller for finding that evidence," Sheriff Jansen said.

The only thing I'd be investigating was which herb or spice would best enhance my new blackberry cordial.

"I promise we're not hanging out a detective shingle," I said. "This is our first and last murder case."

The next day, Toni and I visited Larry Lewis and his wife. She said he'd paid sixty thousand dollars to the blackmailers. It felt good to pay him back. It seemed like their marriage was on the mend.

It was more than I could say for my marriage. The last communication I'd had with Bryan was when I asked him to deposit the rest of Beverly's money into the trust account for Hannah. I didn't give him details when he asked where the money came from, and he didn't push it. He'd expected money from Beverly. He had his secrets with the ghostly swindler, and now I did, too.

I wished him bon voyage, and I kept the guitar I'd bought him for our anniversary. Maybe I'd take a lesson or two.

The next day was Break Thyme's opening. Considering everything that had happened over the last few weeks, my café was in good shape to receive customers bright and early, except for one thing. The replacement windows in the Cozy Nook hadn't come in yet, but as Poppy suggested after visiting Bookend Bay's local art shop, I'd commissioned the owner, a talented artist, to paint portholes to pretty up the boards.

Ruby, from May Flowers next door, brought over lavender and rosemary trees as well as a dozen potted herbs in white planters. Stamped on each pot were inspiring words like *dare to put your dreams into actions*. Yes, indeed. I'd done just that.

"Thank you, Ruby. These are perfect." I touched the basil leaves, releasing their savory fragrance. "They're cheery and smell great, too."

"You're welcome." Ruby's gaze swept over the café. "I can't believe the improvement in here. It's not one bit recognizable from when the Peppers ran this place."

"I love the way it turned out."

"Speaking of the Peppers, did you hear the talk about Richard Pepper?" she asked.

"No. I try not to listen—"

"He drowned in a hot tub after the Peppers moved to Minnesota, you know. Too bad. He was a good man. He and his wife used to argue a lot and that mother-in-law of his. Oh, she was a piece of work, all right. Always mad as spit about something. If I was the sheriff up there, I'd be looking into Richard's death, and I'd be looking into those two women with suspicion."

Oh, dear. I'd have to be careful around Ruby. She was such a gossip.

"I imagine the authorities are doing their job," I said. "Well, I better get these beautiful plants in place. Thank you again, Ruby."

Later that evening, my kids came by to help with the finishing touches. I'd be smiling for a week from how proud they were of my café.

Before I locked the doors for the night, I did one final check that everything was in place for tomorrow's opening. The Nook looked as cozy and inviting as I'd envisioned, especially with the new plants. Everything was as perfect as it was going to get.

I was proud of myself, but I was also nervous. What if nobody showed up tomorrow? What if people didn't like my specialty drinks? What if people didn't want cozy? What if Beverly wasn't gone for good and finally showed up when I had a café full of customers? I had a few questions for the spirited swindler, but not tomorrow. *Please, not tomorrow.*

I turned out the lights and stopped worrying about what could go wrong.

Everything will be better than you can possibly imagine.

The next morning, Poppy and I arrived at 5 a.m. to bake Lemon Thyme Scones. Grateful for her help and cheerfulness, I felt lucky in every way when it came to my head barista.

With the scones freshly baked and the sweet aroma infusing the café, I unlocked the front door and flipped my sign to open. A lineup of people cheered when I opened the door. *Holy moly!*

Poppy was as efficient in the kitchen as she was serving customers. I'd also hired and trained four more staff, Melanie, Jetti, Ethan and Chloe, who were on deck and bustling. Behind the counter, we got into a rhythm and only crashed into each other half a dozen times.

In the first two hours, we gave away one hundred scones and made too many pots of coffee to count. My artisan drinks were a hit. Especially the Bookend Bay Minted Mule, Blackberry Anise Spritzer, Strawberry Basil Lemonade, and Blackberry Mojitos with Star Anise Cordial. The local jams, jellies, and chutneys I had for sale were nearly depleted by the end of the day.

I'd underestimated how hard it was to be on my feet all day. When the café was finally empty, I quickly flipped the sign announcing we were closed. We still had to clean up, but everyone pitched in, and the café was soon sparkling again. I think I thanked everyone ten times.

"I'd say from the smile on your face, opening day was a success," Poppy said when it was just the two of us. She wiped her hands on her apron. The backs of my hands were red from being in water much of the day. She was right. I couldn't have been happier.

"I hope I didn't run you off your feet," I said, plopping down onto a barstool.

"Not at all," Poppy said. "It was fun. Half the town came through here today. I loved seeing everyone."

"You're good with people, Poppy. I can tell you're well-liked."

There was a knock on the door. I turned to see Toni holding a round plastic container.

Poppy removed her apron. "I'll get the door."

"Then you head home, Poppy. Thank you again for working as hard as you did." I took her apron for the laundry, and when I came out of the kitchen, Toni was putting her container down on the counter.

"How are your feet?" she asked.

I laughed. "Swollen, but it's okay."

"You did good, Quinn. I came by earlier but couldn't get in the door."

"Sorry about that. Actually, I'm not sorry. I'm elated."

"I felt that way, too." She picked up my hand and studied my nails. "What's this?"

I'd gotten the name of my daughter-in-law's manicurist and had tiny coffee cups painted on each fingernail. Chelsea had seemed thrilled that I'd done it.

"Aren't they fabulous?" I said.

"I love them." She lifted the lid from her container to reveal a cake with creamy icing, chocolate shavings, and a sprinkle of nuts.

"Is that my favorite hazelnut torte?"

"It is. With salted date caramel and coconut cream." She reached into her bag and pulled out a bottle of champagne. "And bubbly."

"Oh, man. I'd say you shouldn't have, but I'm glad you did." I got up and went behind the counter to fetch plates and cutlery.

"It's not what you think," Toni said, pushing a candle into the cake.

"Oh? We're not celebrating opening day?"

"Nope. Well, not just that. We have something else to celebrate. I wanted to acknowledge this special moment because I learned it's really important. Do you know why?

I had no idea what she was talking about. "Because it comes with cake?"

"Yes. Good point. And because rituals help people get over losses much faster than doing nothing. Or not having cake."

"Losses, huh." The candle on the cake was the number one.

Toni pushed up the sleeves of her light pink sweater. "Quinn, we've been friends a long time. I know you expected to grow old with Bryan, and now well, things have changed. We can't be certain what the future brings, but we do have expectations, and we sure feel it when they're suddenly gone."

Toni knew this firsthand. When her husband died suddenly, it devastated her on levels I hoped to never experience. For one, I'd not understood what it felt like to have a major hole in my future. Not until now.

"I should have made you cake when Norman died," I said.

She laughed. "You gave me exactly what I needed, space and friendship in perfect doses. I hope I can be as good a friend to you."

"If you keep bringing cake, I don't think you can lose." There was a little catch in my voice.

Toni smiled and lit the candle. "Here's to year one of your new future. We don't know what's coming, but you better believe it's going to be better than you can imagine." My new mantra.

I felt tears welling up. I gave her a quick hug and blew out the candle.

After Toni left, my mother called to see how the opening went and to report that the email scam had duped no more of her friends.

"I'm glad to hear it, Mom. I wish we lived in a world where we didn't have to be constantly on guard against these things. Always vigilant when answering the phone or clicking on a hyperlink." She and her friends were so vulnerable. "Be careful, okay? Don't give anyone your personal information, even if they say they're from the Government or your bank. Call me or the kids, right away."

"You don't have to tell me that," she said. "I'm no fool, Quinn."

"You don't have to be a fool. Scammers are getting creative, so just be aware. I love you, Mom. I don't want you to get hurt."

"I know, peanut. I love you, too."

I felt guilty for not telling her about Bryan. I hadn't told my brother either. Not yet. Telling the kids had been draining enough, and I didn't have the energy. Jordan and

Samantha had taken it as well as could be expected, but it had still been one of the saddest days of my life.

I'd just hung up the phone when I realized I wasn't alone. Beverly drifted into view beside the counter. "Speak of scams and the ghostly grifter appears," I said. "You're back. What happened? Do they not want you in the afterworld, not the upper half, I mean?"

She scoffed. She looked even paler than before. "I'm aware your husband deposited Gunner's money into Hannah's account," she said. "Thank you for making that happen. I didn't know if you would once Bryan received his photos."

I started to say something about how those photos were not incriminating when I realized what she'd just said. "Gunner's money? That three-hundred and twenty-seven thousand dollars was his?"

"He thought so, even though I did all the hard work. It took me years to accumulate it, hiding it right under his nose. I had to double up on the extortions or lie about how much money our victims paid."

I shot her a look of disgust. "Stealing that money got you killed, Beverly, and it was a horrible thing to do to Danielle. You broke her heart."

Beverly shrugged. "I warned her not to fall in love. Besides, money wasn't important to her. The hundred grand she gave me was a minor dip in her wealth."

It was impossible to reason with a narcissist or psychopath, or whatever Beverly was.

"You must have suspected Gunner was the one who killed you."

"I didn't know for sure. I had an enemy or two."

Or ten. I let out my breath. "You could have told me he was a criminal just like you."

"You can judge me all you want, but I had to survive. I was on my own at sixteen. I lived on minimum wage for ten years, and I had nothing. I thought things would get better with Andrew Hill, but they didn't. Profits went back into the business. He was okay living on nothing, but I was sick of it. All those nice homes we fixed up, and we were living in a trailer. I had to get away from there.

"I was okay for a few years, and then I started working for a few unsavory characters. Gunner helped me get away. Gave me a place to lie low and to start over."

I didn't care about her life-of-crime excuses. "Why are you here, Beverly?"

She tilted her head and smiled like a snake. "To say thank you. Tell Bryan he did well. Hannah will have enough to get through vet school and her weasel of a grandfather can't touch her money."

That was the only good to have come out of this. "You can haunt him and tell him yourself. Bryan and I are getting a divorce. Thank you very much."

"You're welcome." She opened her arms, spun around. "You have this. You don't need him. He was receptive to me, you know. The only reason it didn't go further between us was because he probably caught the flash of Gunner's camera. Bryan reconsidered though. He reached out to me that Friday night. If I hadn't been otherwise occupied...who knows. And then it was too late for us. But it all turned out in the end."

"It sure did. Especially for you."

She laughed like it was no consequence to be shot in the back. "Before I leave you for good, I'm going to tell you what's coming. Giving you a heads up is the least I can do after what you did for Hannah."

I just stared at her.

"Remember, I said you have twin auras?"

I tapped my foot.

"Do you know why?" she said.

"Beverly, you do realize I believe nothing you say. I don't care if you see quintuplet auras."

"Oh, you will care. I imagine you've already noticed the benefits, tasks being completed under your nose without your knowledge."

That got my attention. Yes, I'd noticed. "Things like dishes being washed, a painted stone appearing out of nowhere, and a breakfast platter left in my fridge?" No one had admitted to doing these things.

"That sounds exactly right. Oh, Quinn..." Beverly laughed again. "One word of advice. Your life is not going to get easier, so you're going to have to get smarter to handle who's coming your way. You're not going to believe it. Not in a million years."

"What's that supposed to mean? Who's coming?" I asked against my better judgment.

"I'm not going to ruin the surprise. I'll tell you this much—I don't think she's from my world or yours. It's a mystery to be sure. When she arrives, think of me." Beverly faded into nothing.

I stood staring into space, feeling my skin crawl, and hating myself for believing a word of her unwelcome omen.

A rush of heat flared from my solar plexus. I fanned myself until it passed. Screw that deceitful, black-mailing, double-dealing ghost.

I poured a half a glass of champagne and toasted my café, the dream I'd dared to put into action.

Worrying about the future was as useful as dwelling on the past. I knew that, but I also knew something else. Deep in my bones, I felt a change coming that had nothing to do with hot flashes and everything to do with a world I couldn't possibly understand.

Where did that thought come from?

I picked up my knife and cut myself a big chunk of torte. I was strong and resilient. I'd survived a ghost and a cheating husband—more than the average, middle-aged person could boast. Whatever challenges came my way, in this world or whatever world Beverly had dreamed up, I'd survive those, too. After all, I had my family; I had my friends, and I knew where to get the absolute best chocolate cake. I was going to be just fine.

The end.

Thank you for reading A *Spirited Swindler*. I hope you enjoyed it. If you'd like to spend more time with Quinn in

Bookend Bay and see what changes are coming her way, I think you'll enjoy the rest of the books in the series. Here's what happens in Book 2, A *Spirited Double*, available on Amazon.

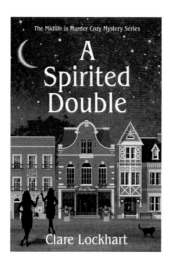

An exorcism gone wrong. An unfathomable other-worldly encounter. And a web of corruption only she can stop.

Recently divorced, Quinn Delaney has enough on her hands trying to win a culinary contest to put her new cafe on the map. One cordial short of an entry, she doesn't have time to help her new renter exorcise an evil spirit from her house.

And then she finds the woman's body face down in her kitchen.

As Quinn begins to unravel the mystery behind her tenant's murder and her brother's sudden avoidance, she suspects something far more sinister is at play in Book-end Bay.

With her best friend Toni by her side, Quinn discovers murder isn't the only ill deed happening in the small town. She soon fears the truth may destroy the people she loves most.

And just when she thinks her life can't get any stranger, she encounters a look-alike visitor with a shocking allegation that turns both their worlds sideways.

Get ready for an adventure where the unexpected will keep you guessing until the very end in this fun and fast-paced paranormal cozy mystery!

To find out what happens next, pick up your copy of A *Spirited Double*!

Did You Get Your Free Book?

I WANT TO THANK you for spending time with Quinn and her challenging midlife. I hope you had fun reading this mystery and would like to know what's happening next in Quinn's world.

Can we stay in touch?

If you had fun with Quinn and her friends in Bookend Bay, I invite you to join my newsletter here or on my website **https://clarelockhart.com** and get a **FREE** novella in the series. In my newsletter, I'll let you know about new book releases, book discounts, promotions featuring other cozy mysteries, news about the books I'm working on next, a few personal stories, and fun giveaways.

Or if you'd rather not join the newsletter and just be notified of the next book release, follow me on Amazon and/or Bookbub.

Happy reading!

Love and hugs,

Clare

Acknowledgements

First, I want to thank Megan Records for your helpful edits. Also thank you to Wanda for your input, encouragement and edits regarding the opening of the story.

And a big thank you to my critique group: Carole Ann Vance, Linda Farmer, Sheila Tucker and Norma Meldrum, for your ongoing insightful edits and for sticking with me and my endeavors for many years, especially over the last two years when we've had to meet outdoors or by video conferencing to stay safe through the pandemic.

I also want to thank Irene Jorgensen for your helpful suggestions and for all the brainstorming sessions we do, especially the ones on the beach. I'm convinced sand and water help to boost creativity!

A special thank you to Megan Bernas, chef extraordinaire, who is always available to provide food and café details. And to Ashley Christian, a meticulous beta reader, who finds little details that make a big difference.

And to John Burrows for being my champion, for helping me plot (fictional) murder, and for being my chief proofreader. I will be forever grateful for your rabbit-hole searches and never-ending enthusiasm.

About the Author

Clare Lockhart grew up on Nancy Drew and paranormal stories from her dad who loved all things supernatural. She writes light-hearted, small-town, paranormal cozy mysteries featuring middle-aged sleuths who are going through a few changes. If you like reading about best friends who find themselves in the odd pickle, twisty murder plots that keep you guessing, and cheeky, paranormal visitors, then you'll love these fast-paced mysteries!

She would love to hear from you, so please send an email to clare@clarelockhart.com and visit https://clarelockhart.com/ to learn more about Clare and her books.

If you'd like to receive A FREE BOOK IN THE SERIES, hear the latest news, and stay in touch, please join Clare Lockhart's mailing list on her website.

Manufactured by Amazon.ca
Acheson, AB

14155645R00144